An Unexpected Friendship

Amherstburg 1846

JANE BUTTERY

Copyright © 2010 by Jane Buttery.

Library of Congress Control Number: 2010915216
ISBN: Hardcover   978-1-4535-9379-0
          Softcover   978-1-4535-9378-3
          Ebook   978-1-4535-9380-6

All rights reserved. No part of this book may be reproduced or transmitted in any form or by any means, electronic or mechanical, including photocopying, recording, or by any information storage and retrieval system, without permission in writing from the copyright owner.

This is a work of fiction. Names, characters, places and incidents either are the product of the author's imagination or are used fictitiously, and any resemblance to any actual persons, living or dead, events, or locales is entirely coincidental.

This book was printed in the United States of America.

Other Books by the same author

If I could go to the Harrow Fair
A Cookie for the Christ Child
Let's go to Colasanti's
Mei Ling Discovers Jack Miner
Portraits of an Orchestra
No says I love you. I A Safe Day with
Explorer Sam
I know the rules. Do You? II Safe from the Fire with
Explorer Sam
The Community of Faith centred on Christ Church 1805-2005

To order additional copies of this book, contact:
Xlibris Corporation   or   TRUELIGHT
1-888-795-4274   519-738-4708
www.Xlibris.com   www.truestorybooks.com
Orders@Xlibris.com

Table of Contents

Chapter 1 An Accidental Meeting ....page 1
Chapter 2 Seamus at home 5
Chapter 3 A Visit to the Store 9
Chapter 4 Josh's Unpleasant Encounter 15
Chapter 5 Mr. Fry Explains 19
Chapter 6 Seamus Makes Some Discoveries 23
Chapter 7 Josh at the Dougall School 27
Chapter 8 Meetings after School 31
Chapter 9 Seamus' Lucky Day 37
Chapter 10 Josh visits His Family 41
Chapter 11 Seamus Fights Back 47
Chapter 12 Summer Jobs 51
Chapter 13 More Developments 55
Chapter 14 Exciting news for Seamus 61
Chapter 15 Disturbing News for Josh 67
Chapter 16 Bad news for the Maloney Family 71
Chapter 17 December Meeting 75
Chapter 18 The Concert 79
Chapter 19 Fire at the Dock 83
Chapter 20 Learning 89
Chapter 21 A New Experience 93
Chapter 22 All on Board 99
Chapter 23 Two Families Reunited 105
Chapter 24 The Journey Home to Amherstburg 109
A Note about the people in this book 115
Reference Books 117

For Brian, Richard and Matthew Buttery with my love

Acknowledgements

My thanks go to our librarian Cathy Humphrey for her help and support and to the Marsh Collection and Fort Malden's Resources in Amherstburg for their fine collection of local documents. The Harrow Early Immigrant Resource Library has extensive local censuses as well as much information about early settlements which was invaluable. I appreciate Edith Woodbridge's knowledge of local history. I particularly thank Loetta Brndjar for the time she gave editing this manuscript in detail. Finally I am fortunate to have a patient husband Brian who has given me useful suggestions.

Jane Buttery

Map of Amherstburg in 1846

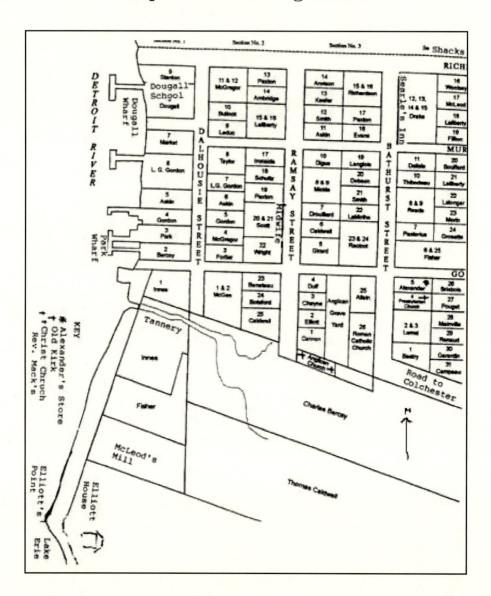

Chapter 1

An Accidental Meeting

On a warm April morning in 1846, twelve year old Josh Stokes hurried along the roadway towards the Elliott house. "What if that Billy Warton comes after me?" he thought. Not daring to look around, he gripped a big crock full of maple syrup that he was hauling across to the big house east of town for old Mrs. Elliott. Would he get it there safely? Delivering goods for Uncle Alexander was one way to get out of the dusty general store. Josh used to enjoy walking beside the Detroit River as it meandered out of Amherstburg but he no longer felt safe since Billy was pestering him all the time. His boots sank into the pools of slushy snow and his heavy pants were now splattered with mud. He'd never be able to escape the Warton gang carrying this crock! Then he smiled as he thought of his father's words. "Never forget, Josh, you be a free man here. You get some learnin', go far and stand up for yourself. That's why I got us all out of that there plantation in Kentucky. Don't you forget it."

Of course Josh never forgot but he still wanted to avoid meeting that bully, Billy. If only he had a real friend in town! He heaved a sigh and stopped to put the crock down. Just then Josh noticed a taller thin boy in tattered pants idly kicking at stones by the McLeod Mill. 'Wonder who he is?' Josh thought. 'I haven't seen him in town before. Perhaps he'd be friendly.' He watched as a burley man approached the boy, said something to him and cuffed him on the shoulder. When the man moved away, the boy turned his gaunt face to the man's back and stuck out his tongue. Then, hugging his jacket to him against a sudden sharp breeze, the boy kicked furiously at a stone. This time, it flew and hit the back of Josh's leg.

Josh winced, "Hey there. No need to take it out on me", shouted Josh, putting the jar down to rub his ankle. "Oh . . . didn't mean nothing," the boy replied in a sharp voice with an accent that was hard to follow. "Pity it didn't hit that one who pushed me!"

"Lucky for you it didn't. He's Mr. McLeod's foreman."

"You seem to know a lot. I'll come over", replied the boy starting across the muddy road. Then he added, "I'm new here. But who're you to be telling me'self what to do?"

"Keep calm. Just meant to help. I'm Josh Stokes. What's your name?"

"The name's Seamus Maloney from Cork, Ireland. Your man back there says there's no work for the likes of me! But I'm almost fourteen and stronger than I look," he added, shaking his fist in the air.

At that Josh looked up at Seamus and saw a very thin lanky boy with a long pale face and thin straight hair. 'He looks in need of a good meal!' Josh thought but said, "Well, Seamus, I've this syrup to deliver," as he picked up the heavy jug. Seamus started to move away off but Josh suggested, "Want to come along with me?"

"Might as well for now. You going somewhere special?" Seamus asked.

"Just delivering this to the big house for my uncle," Josh replied acknowledging the load under his chin.

Seamus nodded and clumped along the bumpy wet road after Josh in silence. Some minutes later, the two saw the big brick home with its long sweep of grass going down to the river.

"That's the Elliott home," said Josh pointing to the house. "Real nice isn't it?"

"What'd they do to deserve that? Trample over poor people?" demanded Seamus

"What makes you say that?" Josh stopped, put down his load and turned to face him. "You sure get sore easily!"

The boy turned and stomped off. Then he shouted back, "I don't need the likes of you to tell me off. You don't know what it's like to lose your home."

An Unexpected Friendship

Josh didn't want to spoil a chance to make a new friend. "Sorry, Seamus. Didn't mean to hurt you! Stay here. I won't be long at the house and we can walk back to town together."

"Maybe I will. Maybe I won't," the boy replied, leaning against the huge trunk of an elm tree.

Josh picked up the jug and went round to the back door where he found his Ma's friend Sadie putting out washing. He was glad to put his awkward load down at last on a nearby stump.

"Nice day, Josh," she said cheerfully. "You got some new syrup for Missus Elliott?"

"Yes. I sure have and it's real heavy. Mr. Botsford brought it down to the store and asked me to deliver it right quick."

"Well, you did good," Sadie commented." "Bring it in," she added opening the heavy pine door.

Inside the big kitchen the smell of fresh bread filled the air. Josh swallowed when he put the crock down on the kitchen floor. He often got a taste of Sadie's cooking.

"Sit yourself down and have some apple cider, Josh. Here's a biscuit too."

"That's right kind of you, Sadie but I can't stay. Met a new boy and don't want to let him alone."

"Well that's real nice for you, Josh. Drink up and, here," she stopped to get another biscuit off the big slab near the stove, "Take him a biscuit too."

"Thanks, Sadie. I know he can use it. He looks mighty hungry. I'll see you. Bye."

"Come again, Josh. It's good to see your cheerful face round here. Tell your auntie I'll be by to see her come Sunday."

"I sure will," Josh answered as he hurried across the wet grass looking to see if Seamus was still around. He wasn't by the elm anymore; but Josh spotted him as he sauntered along the high ground by the river. Everyone called it Elliott's Point because it was near the big house Robert Elliott had built in 1835.

"Hey," Josh shouted. "Wait for me."

The boy turned around and before he could speak, Josh gave him a biscuit. "My friend Sadie said to give you one."

The boy mumbled, "Uh . . . thanks." Then he smelt the fresh dough and ate slowly.

"Like that?" Josh inquired after a while.

"Yes. You got nice friends."

"Yep. Sadie's my ma's friend from way back in Kentucky. She's the best cook, I know."

For the first time, Seamus smiled. "So you come from somewhere else too . . . like me."

"We come from way down south but I was too little to remember. We escaped to Canada ten years ago and Sadie came with us."

"Escaped?" the boy quizzed looking at Josh with interest. "Why?"

"All of us were slaves and I know that's wrong. A nice man came round the plantation and told my Pa what to do to get to Canada." Josh stopped and added with pride what he'd heard so often, "My Pa wanted us to be free."

The boy's eyes lit up as he said, "My Da worked for a big fancy Englishman. I hated him 'cause he drove us out of our house when we'd no money and no food. Another man found us passage on a boat here. My sister and brother died on the way out."

"That's awful, man! What trouble you've had," Josh replied

"Indeed I have but I won't be beat. Me and you've something in common. Put it there, Josh," he added, offering his hand.

"Glad we met, Seamus," Josh replied. "Come see me at Alexander's Store on the Gore."

"I will do that," Seamus agreed. The two boys slapped hands together and raced along the river bank to Amherstburg.

A view of the waterfront in Amherstburg

Chapter 2

Seamus at home

Seamus was still excited as he went into the smoky shack to find his mother. He had a new friend and he wanted to share his good fortune with her. But he stopped when he saw her bending over to reach a pot, wiping her thin arm over her forehead. Dermot stood close by and his sister Mary sat coughing on the stool. Seamus noted his mother's fine brown hair was already grey in parts. She turned to face him and demanded, "And where have you been this long time, my boy?" Seamus, lost for words, could only shake his head and look at his feet.

"Well?" his mother added. "Have you no tongue in your head? Don't you know I need help around here now your Da is working?" She returned to stirring the last of the oatmeal into the old pot that hung across the smoky fire.

"Sorry, Mam. I tried to find work. No luck but I met another boy who works in a store. What do you want me to do?"

"Don't let that happen again! We need fresh water. You can eat after you get it."

All this time two year old Dermot was pulling on her long black skirt.

"Come on Dermot I'll take you out with me and play you a tune," Seamus offered.

"You'll not be playing any tunes at this hour of the day, Seamus Maloney! There's chores to be done. Take the bucket now and our

Mary can go with you. Dermot needs his food." Then she bent down, picked up the child, kissing him on the forehead.

"I'll go, Mam and be back soon." Seamus turned to his sister, "Come, Mary I'll play you a song about old Ireland on the way there."

"Now off with you! I need peace," his mother commanded. "Mary, take my warm shawl to go." Mary wrapped her thin body in the lovely woven shawl, her mother had made. She seemed smaller than her seven years; her big green eyes looked at him eagerly. The green and dark blues of the shawl gave her pale skin some colour. She followed Seamus outside but, within seconds, the cool air started her coughing again. She worried Seamus. He put the bucket over one arm and gave her a hug. "Here, I'll play you a jolly tune like grandpa did."

Seamus' tin whistle soon filled the air. As seven year old Mary trotted along side him, his mind went back to his grandfather in Ireland and the happy times he had had learning from him. The old man was too sick to come with them last year and the whistle had been his gift to Seamus with the words, "Now you promise me to keep it up. You'll be knowing when it's good to play."

Seamus played on, happily remembering his beloved grandfather. He noticed that Mary was no longer coughing; she was skipping to his music. When they reached the well, the little girl smiled up at her big brother.

"That's a fine pipe you play," said a strong voice behind them. "Reminds me of the times we had at Searle's Inn a while back. Never hear music there now."

Seamus looked round to see an older man coming alongside them. He had a rugged outdoor look; his strong muscles showed through his shirt. He went on in a friendly voice, "You must be from around Cork with music like that coming out of you."

Seamus was so surprised that he dropped the bucket. Picking it up quickly, he replied in a rush of words, "We are indeed. How do you know it so well, sir?"

"Well now wouldn't I? My own brother's still living there. A grand place!" the man exclaimed with a twinkle in his eye.

"Maybe once but not now!" replied Seamus, his body suddenly tensed. "There's naught to eat and no work. My da had us leave there while we could. Our potatoes had the blight."

An Unexpected Friendship

"I heard that from my brother. It's that sorry I am you had to face it. A hard life we had there. I'm glad I came six years back." Then he said more cheerfully, "Is this your sister? Any more pretty ones like her at home?"

"No. Mary's my only sister now and little Dermot. We lost my older sister and a brother on the long sea trip with the fever."

"Oh, 'tis a terrible shame. You've had your share of troubles." Patting Mary's head, he added," My name's Michael Maloney. I have a blacksmith's place down the Gore but I want to get farming more. Let me know if I can help."

Seamus and Mary both chuckled before they said, "Our name's Maloney too."

"We live over there for now," Seamus added, pointing down the road to their small place.

"Oh, do you now? I've land north of the Texas Road. You ask your da to look for me at the Inn. I usually go down there of an evening."

"I will that," Seamus agreed. "My da works at the livery stables nearby now."

"Good for him. Now let me fill the bucket while you give me another tune."

Seamus was only too pleased to oblige and he noted that Mary hadn't coughed since they fell in with Mr. Maloney. He played a favourite jig before they said goodbye and headed home.

"Mammy, Mammy, we met a nice man," Mary called excitedly.

"He liked Seamus' tunes and his name's Maloney!"

"Well now, isn't that a surprise," her mother replied. "What does he do, Seamus?"

"He's a blacksmith and he has a farm too. He told me to tell Da to look him up."

"Oh, that's interesting. Come now and eat up this oatmeal. Then Seamus I'll have you go to get some more food for me at a store."

This gave Seamus the opportunity to talk about Josh. "Mam, the boy I met today works at his uncle's store and he was that kind to me. He's a coloured boy called Josh Stokes. Can I go there? They have new syrup just in. Can we get some?"

"Coloured? Perhaps they'd be more friendly than some of these white folk who look down on us Irish."

"Now Ma, Da has a job and things will get better. Can I get some food for you?"

"Why not? Tomorrow maybe when your da brings some money. I'll make a list for you to take. Finish up your food. It's plain but good for you. I know we need salt, flour, potatoes, butter and sugar. I'll buy a little meat now your da has work."

"That's good Mam. I'll go for you first thing." Seamus pushed down the rest of the thin oatmeal and sat back. Remembering Mr. Maloney, he said boldly, "That's two new people I've met in one day! Maybe our luck will change now Mam."

"Maybe," she mouthed. But she seemed miles away as she stared out the door.

Seamus took up the bowls and washed them as his mother made a list. She'd come from a good family and learned to read and write. When she had time, she'd started to teach Seamus his letters but he'd forgotten so much in the past two hard years.

"I'm too tired to think now Seamus. I may think of more tomorrow. You'll be needing a can for the flour too. Mind you no dawdling tomorrow!"

"I won't Mam." With the list in his pocket, Seamus looked round for other jobs he needed to do. "I'll gather some more sticks Mam to keep us warm."

When she smiled at him, he felt good. Tomorrow, he would have a chance to see Josh again.

This is a typical 19th century general store like the one James Alexander may have had.

Chapter 3

A Visit to the Store

Josh awoke to the sound of a cat's mournful 'meow' and the grunting of two old hogs in the barn. Even though the straw scratched the back of his neck, he was reluctant to move from underneath the heavy comforting patchwork quilt. The thin gray light of early April barely warmed this rough room above the store but he couldn't linger in bed. Aunt Corrie's voice came strong and powerful,

"Josh, you be down here now and sweep out this store afore it's open." He grabbed his old britches from the cold floor and struggled into them under the quilt. Soon he smelt the inviting aroma of hot oatmeal waiting up the stairs. Like a ruffled bear cub, he emerged onto the bare boards, hearing his pa's words again,

"You be lucky, staying with Aunt Corrie and your Uncle Jim so you can learn. Don't you forget that. We be free now and we got to show we be as good as any white man." Those words suited Josh who loved to have his head in books; he savoured the smoothness of their silky pages.

Learning was his real love; chores were a necessity! He rushed down to the warm room below, taking in the fragrance of coffee brewing on the hob and anticipating the sweet taste of oatmeal with fresh maple syrup. He felt his aunt's fingers run through his thick black curly hair and onto his shoulder as she gently pushed him towards the dusty store.

Some hours later, Josh was rolling a barrel of flour into the store when Seamus almost ran into him.

"Hey there. Watch out! I've got to put this barrel in place!" Josh exclaimed, grinning as he turned. "We always seem to meet with a bang, Seamus!"

"Sorry, Josh. My mam needs some things. She said no dawdling. Here's her list."

"Fine, I'll help you now. Just let me put this into place," Josh replied, setting the heavy barrel down. Seamus was amazed that such a small boy could handle that weight. As if he heard Seamus' thoughts, Josh said rubbing his hands against a long white apron,

"You know I'm beginning to see how to handle that barrel now. It's as much skill as being tough!"

Seamus smiled and looked around at the shelves full of different sized jars, big crocks and shiny tins. It was fun to look at all the different goods. Big wooden barrels holding corn meal and flour stood up against the counters on the sawdust strewn floor. There were pots, pans, tools and bolts of blue and black cloth on one counter. 'How I'd love to get some for my mam! Maybe one day,' he thought while he warmed his hands by the pot bellied stove.

Josh came over to the counter and said, "Just read your list to me and I'll get what you need."

There was silence before Seamus, looking down at the floor, admitted, "Can't read. But Mam said to get flour, salt, meat and some of that syrup you have for the oatmeal. Oh! And some butter if you have some."

"We do have some over there," Josh said pointing to a cold white slab covered with cheese cloth. Seamus put the list on the counter, his thin face full of worry as he twisted his cap in his hands.

Picking up the paper, Josh said, "Right. Two pounds of flour, some tea, one cup of syrup, oatmeal, potatoes, a quarter of salt, a half pound of butter and pork. Sorry, no potatoes-they didn't keep well. I'll give you a squash. Good taste. I'll get the flour first from from the new barrel."

Josh took a big scoop and the tin Seamus gave him. As he weighed the container using a small weight, Seamus recognised a big 2 on it.

"It's just over two ounces," commented Josh. "I'll put the fl our in now." He filled the tin to the brim. Dusting off his hands on his

An Unexpected Friendship

long white apron, he weighed it on the scales. It was over two pounds by three ounces. All the time, Seamus watched the scales trying to learn the weights when Josh measured out sugar, butter and salt. Just then a large black man came in, smiling broadly. "Mornin', son. Haven't seen you afore. I'm Josh's uncle Alexander."

"I'm Seamus. We've been here ever since we come afore winter."

"And you didn't need no food?" Mr Alexander teased.

"We got food given us. Didn't have much money," Seamus muttered. Then he lifted his head up, his face brighter. "Now my da's got work at a stable and we've got some."

"That's good. Now Josh, are you getting what the boy wants?"

"Yes Uncle, but I haven't measured out a cup of syrup yet."

"Then, I'll do that," said his uncle. Seamus watched the tall black man's big hands pull down a large crock and measure out the right amount. "We'll lend you a small jar. Bring it back next time," he said as he put the crock back on a high shelf behind him. "Where'd you live, Seamus?"

"We got one of the shacks off a street called Richmond."

"I know the place. Has your father cleared any land yet?"

"He tried to dig the bit of what we got round us—enough to put in potatoes, turnips and cabbage but he says the ground's still too hard."

"That's true enough," replied Mr. Alexander. "He'll find he can get them in another two weeks or more. It's not like England here boy."

"We're not English!" Seamus protested, sticking his chest out.

"We're Irish from Cork."

"Sorry I made a wrong guess. You do sound different from some. I don't know about places over there." Then Mr. Alexander added more gently, "We're just glad to help. Anyway, if your dad needs shovel or hoe, I can lend him one when the time comes."

Seamus, twisted his cap in his hands and smiled up at the kind black face. "I'll tell him. Sure it's wonderful kind you are!" Then he added, wanting to offer something in return, "My da's good with animals if you have any."

"Thank you. If we'd known you had needs, son, we'd have helped you. I'll just cut you a bit of this salted pork. Now Seamus," he said putting his hands down on counter, "You got some money there? I added your goods up and it comes to seven and a half pennies."

"I've got that and more," Seamus said, proudly counting out the pennies. His thin face lit up with pleasure. "Mam'll love that pork too. It's a fair time since we had any. Is that all to pay?"

"That's enough, now," Mr. Alexander smiled and added, "The salted pork's a welcome gift. We have plenty to share."

"Here're your goods, Seamus and a squash to try," Josh added.

"Can you manage all this?"

"Sure I can," Seamus stated but, as he picked up the uneven bundles, the squash fell to the floor.

"Let's see now," said Josh's uncle, picking up the squash. "We could put it in one sack . . . but better if you go along, Josh and help. I wouldn't want him spilling that syrup or the tea."

"Can I? I won't be long, Uncle. Then I'll know 'xactly where Josh lives."

"Right. You do that."

"Thank you, sir. My mam will be right thankful and have me come here again."

"Well Alexander's General Store is here to serve," finished Mr. Alexander with a hearty laugh.

Josh took off his apron, hanging it carefully on a big hook. He picked up the tin of flour, the salt and tea while Seamus took the sack of oatmeal and the jar of syrup.

"Come on, Seamus and show me the way." The boys walked out into the warm sunshine on Bathurst Street, smiling as they carried the bundles of food.

A Picture of old Amherstburg in about 1860 in the Public domain. Note the unpaved streets and the wooden sidewalk near a horse and carriage.

Chapter 4

Josh's Unpleasant Encounter

"This way," Seamus commanded, moving ahead on the narrow streets. Long shadows from the many tall trees coming into bud, cast their huge outlines across the deep ruts in the street. More snow had melted during the day and a horse-drawn cart came by, splashing the boys' pants.

They had to go one behind the other as they crossed Murray Street. Two prim white ladies stared at them and one commented pointedly,

"There's that coloured boy consorting with our kind."

"They need to know their place, I say," said the other in a louder voice.

Josh's small body stiffened at the remarks but Seamus turned round and glared at the women. They turned away and the boys went on. Soon Josh was stopped by an older black lady, shaking out a mat. "Hi there, Josh. School over yet?"

"No, Missus Hurst. In another two weeks."

"Well, you go on learnin', Josh. Your mama'll be proud of you!"

"Thank you, Missus Hurst. I will."

Seamus stopped and looked sharply at Josh. "You go to school still? I thought you just worked in the store."

"I help my uncle and aunt 'cause they have me stay when school's on. I go to the Dougall School down by the dock. Mr. Peden teaches us."

"Do you like all that learning?"

"Of course. My pa says it's important. He had to learn to read secretly but I can go to school!"

"Secretly? Why?"

"Well my Pa told us that slaves weren't allowed to learn. The white folk said they weren't good enough but that's not true. They just kept us down that way."

"Really?" Seamus quizzed wrinkling up his nose. "So aren't you the lucky one. I never had a chance at regular school—too much to do," he whined, looking away from Josh as they headed up Richmond. Josh was silent, wondering, 'Did Seamus want to learn to read? Maybe he could help him. He'd have to think about it.'

Just at that instant something hard hit his back. He turned to see Billy Warton's ginger hair as he ran behind a tree. Seamus stopped and saw Josh stoop down, balancing the tin and sack against his knees. "You all right?" asked Seamus.

But just then he heard, "Get lost, slimy coloured!" Meanwhile Josh was rubbing the back of his neck without saying a word.

"What's that kid up to?" Seamus asked, "He hit you. I saw him running off."

"Just some bully from school who likes picking on me," Josh explained. "Forget it."

"We can fight back, Josh or he'll do it again."

"He's not worth it. Let's get your mother's food to her."

"I have to or I'd stop and fight him now. Why do you let him treat you that way?"

Josh said nothing but thought that Billy and his gang were becoming more of a menace every time he walked down the street. He knew he should be braver and Seamus could help but he hated a fight. All Josh wanted was peace to do his work at school and to help with the store.

Walking side by side, the two boys passed by three more log cabins and two shacks. Soon Seamus saw his sister by an open door and ran to her. She looked about seven to Josh and her grey dress clung to her thin body. She eyed Josh for a moment as Seamus spoke.

"I've got the food Mammy wanted, Mary. This is my friend, Josh from the store." Mary looked at him shyly but, with another brief glance at Josh, she ran inside, calling, "Mammy, food." Josh waited till Seamus took his bundle and the syrup in.

An Unexpected Friendship

After a moment he returned, saying, "Thanks Josh. We've not much room inside or I'd have you come in. Mam thanks your uncle for the pork."

"Glad to help, Seamus. I must get back to the store. Goodbye for now."

"Bye Josh. And watch out for that pea-shooter."

"Pea-shooter? Yes. Perhaps that's what Billy used. Bye."

Josh strode back down Richmond, looking to see if Billy was still around. He just wanted to get back safely to the store. But it wasn't long before Billy, pushing his cap down on his thick ginger hair, came up in front of him. This time, he was joined by the Innes boys who stood head and shoulders taller than Josh. Together, they barred his way. There was no escape.

"What you up to, Boy?" Billy demanded, clenching his fists in front of Josh's face. "I saw you making up to that skinny new 'un. Think he could protect you, do you? What a laugh! He's all skin and bones, right boys?"

"Yes, Billy and Josh is Mr. Peden's pet! We've watched you trying to get as clever as us. As if you could!" exclaimed Duncan Innes. Josh just sucked in his lip, trying not to show how scared he felt inside.

"We know what you're trying to do! Borrowing books from Peden and making us look bad. Go and do your learning somewhere else. We don't need you coloureds in our school!"

"Yeah! Josh Stokes. Get out of our school!" added David Innes, pushing Josh against a tree.

"You watch it, you little shrimp!" scowled the taller Duncan Innes.

"My father says we should'na have to sit with you coloureds in the same room so take that," he added kicking Josh in the shin with his heavy boot.

Josh cowered by the tree; he was pinned in by the three of them. He saw no way out.

"We're warning you," added Billy. "Get out now or it'll be the worse for you."

"And don't think no scrawny Irish's goin' help you," added Duncan.

Turning to his taller pals, Billy threatened, "Let's teach him a lesson boys."

Josh dropped to the ground as he eyed Billy's menacing look, wondering how he could get away. This time he was in luck. They all heard a cart rumbling towards them. As they turned round, they saw Mr. Fry was driving towards them. Josh made a move to run past the boys but Billy stuck his leg out and Josh fell into the grimy slush. All three boys laughed.

"That's nothing to laugh at. Now git," shouted Mr. Fry, slapping his whip on the side of his cart. The boys scurried off as he turned to Josh, "You all right, Josh? Did those rascals hurt you?"

"Not much. Just threatening me as usual!" he replied rubbing off his knees.

"I knows they are and they're not the only ones in town! We got to stick together Josh. You look mighty shook up. Come with me and I'll drop by your uncle's."

"Thanks, I promised to be back real quick," Josh replied.

"Well, git up 'ere and we'll be off." With that comment, Mr. Fry headed up Apsley Street towards Gore and back to Josh's uncle's store on the next corner.

Minutes later, Josh got off the cart and was about to thank Mr. Fry when he said, "I'm coming in. I saw some of that and I didn't like the looks of it! 'Bout time we did something."

Chapter 5

Mr. Fry Explains

Mr Fry tied his horse up out front and marched behind Josh into his uncle's store, calling out, "Jim, you in there? Need to speak to you!"

Mr. Alexander took one look at Josh all muddied up and said,

"What happened out there this time?"

"I saw some of it Jim. Those Innes boys egged on by that Billy Warton, were giving Josh a rough time."

"Not again! They really seem to have it in for Josh even though they go to his school."

"That's the trouble, uncle. They don't like me getting an education like them. They said their father didn't like me being in their school."

"Can't believe that. Mr. Innes is right civil with me. I buy from him, Tom." Josh's uncle stated.

"I'm not surprised Jim. We all of us facing some problems like this. Some of these merchants don't mind me doing some carting and fetching for them but won't give me the regular paying jobs out of town." Mr. Fry sat down, rubbing his callused hands round his chin. "We got to help when those ruffians start attacking our boys. My Henry's had trouble with 'em. Maybe we do need our own school."

"That's just what they'd like us to do, Tom. No. I think I must talk to Mr. Dougall. He's a fair man and it was his idea to have the school. We need to get along with each other. That's the future, Tom."

"Maybe it is but I won't have Henry suffer from the likes of the Innes and Warton boys. No siree! We have rights here in Canada. Josh's father served the militia in the past and got his land fair. Josh can stand up proud of Peter Stokes and of you Jim."

Josh's mouth dropped open at these words. This story was new to him! He'd been too small when it all happened. He was finding out how much all the coloured men knew of the feelings in the town. What was this militia? He was curious: here was a chance to find out some things.

"I knew my dada had free land, Mr. Fry but I never understood why."

"Well now, son. That's some story but I've done my job fer today and I've a mind to tell you."

"Sit yourself down there by the stove, Tom and I'll get you a good hot coffee," suggested Josh's uncle. "Go wash up Josh, come right back and listen."

Within minutes Josh returned, his hands and face clean and his apron on. "All right? Now Josh, you clean that lower shelf and keep the tea next to the coffee and spices," his uncle said. "Right, Tom, tell us the old story. I've never told him or my young John."

"Right then? I'll begin." With that Mr. Fry tapped out his clay pipe, stuffed in tobacco and lit it.

"It was early on January the eighth of '38, a freezing cold day and all. There'd be trouble down east so they asked us to join the militia.

We'd joined under Captain Caldwell—about 30 of us—even old Josiah Henson and Moses Brantford. Early that morn, someone sighted the rebels bringing the schooner Anne down the icy river. But it was no ordinary run. No Siree! She had canon on board and was firing at the town just past the fort. We heard the boom, boom and our militia came together quickly. We's soon ready as she sailed down near Elliott's Point. There was no way we'd let those slave-owning 'Mericans land here! We got our arms ready to fight. One of our men fired across the water and got the man at the rudder. It was a dead hit! The boat came towards the shore and a few of us waded into the icy waters. We captured the lot of them! Aye, that was a proud day indeed. We took them prisoners. Right Jim?"

"Yes, there'd be 'bout twenty. The soldiers from the fort came after. But it's your story, Tom. Go on." Josh turned round to see his uncle leaning against the counter, arms folded as he listened. It was an exciting story to know, Josh thought. Mr. Fry warmed his hands and went on.

"Well, the soldiers be coming along after us men secured the prisoners. I reckon we saved the day right enough! Your Dada did his bit, Josh, like the rest of us. That's how he got the land as a reward. Matt Matthew's got some too in the new settlement. It was a proud day for us all," Mr. Fry added, looking upwards as though he could picture the whole scene. Then he finished, "We felt wanted in those days, not like today. They soon forget that we chose to fight alongside them."

"Well, I won't," said Josh. "That's the best story I've heard about my dada and all of you. Wonder why he never told me it."

"Your dada's not one to brag, Josh. Quiet man. A proud farmer glad to have land."

"Thanks for telling me that, Mr. Fry. I'll stand up for my right to learn even more. I'm not leaving school!"

"That's the spirit, Josh. You and Henry will make a good pair at school." With that, he got off the old chair. "Must be off and feed that horse of mine afore supping."

"Thank you, Mr. Fry for bringing me back."

"No trouble. Any time I be passing."

Chapter 6

Seamus Makes Some Discoveries

About a week later, Seamus decided to try his hand at fishing. His da liked fish to eat. He stripped some small branches off a nearby tree and found some old twine. Sitting outside, he prepared his makeshift line. Then he thought of bait. The ground was getting warmer so he tried scraping at it with a piece of loose board. After working for a few minutes, he spotted a couple of wiggly worms. Taking an old tin can he put in the worms and worked at getting more. Dermot had toddled out and was soon asking questions,
"What they be, Seamus? Me touch them?"
"They be squiggly worms, Dermot. Feel one." Dermot took it and was about to try it with his tongue. "Oh no. Don't be doing that now. You'll sick up!" Seamus warned. "Now come in to Mammy. I'm gonna catch us some fish." Taking his little brother inside, Seamus pronounced proudly, "I've made a fishing line, Mam and I'm off to fish. I can catch us some supper."
"Perhaps you will and all. Your grandpa liked to fish and you have his ways about you. Go on then," she said, realizing this older son tried to shoulder many responsibilities.
Seamus took off down Richmond to the river and was soon passing the dock and Josh's School. He tried reading a sign but could only make out odd letters. 'If I had some help,' he thought. 'I'd learn fast.

I know I could get better work if I could read. If only Mam had more time to show me my letters again!'

Then his eye caught a big schooner coming into the dock. Men were waiting to unload her. The ice had broken up now and there was more happening on the river. In the distance, he saw steam coming out into the air. He stopped to watch and soon saw the steamer Anchor coming in from Sandusky. There were people on board looking out at the town. Seamus sat down just past the dock and watched.

In a short while, the steamer pulled in further down from the schooner Thomas F. Park and planks were laid down to let people off. To his amazement Seamus watched two black men practically run down the gang-plank and drop to their knees, crying, "We's here in the promised land! We be free now brother!" They got up and turned round to face three more of their family; a tall thin woman carrying one child and followed by another, came carefully down the plank. "God be praised, Jeremiah. We be here at last."

Soon a black man with a broad smile and kindly face came to greet them. "Welcome to Canada. Now you come with me and we'll give you some help." The small group followed him away from the dock but Seamus overheard the talk that followed.

"That be the fifth family to come in. Why we be letting all those coloureds in here?"

"It's that Henry Bibb and his abolitionists," grumbled another.

"There ought to be a law to control them!"

"Now, Jim," said a woman standing nearby. "We got to let them have a chance. We're all God's children"

"But some of us not be a burden, Missus." The man turned round to pull away the planks and saw Seamus.

"And what you staring at, Irish? I've seen ya' hanging round. You're just a load of trouble too!" That made Seamus jump up and run out of the town towards the place Josh showed him. He remembered it was quiet and today, he didn't want trouble. He walked quickly past the mill and along the bank until he came near the big house. 'There's the spot that goes out. I'll try my luck there,' he thought.

He flopped down on the cold grass, almost out of breath. Soon he attached his bait and swung his line out into the water. He'd seen plenty of small whitefish the day he'd waited for Josh. Now he'd catch some. As if to charm the fish, he began to play a quiet sad tune. Soon he felt a tugging on the line and he pulled in his first fish. Then, he put on more bait and sat down to wait. Feeling happier, he put more into his playing trying to remember the old song, A Gentle Harpe,[1] he once knew.

He was so engrossed in it that he did not hear the rustle of ladies' gowns behind him. Putting his tin whistle down to try the line, he almost fell over as he heard a lady's voice over his shoulder. "And what are you doing at my point, young man?"

Seamus dropped the pole as he fumbled around, "Just fishing, Ma'am. Didn't know I couldn't."

"Then you must be new here and I can tell that you're from old Ireland. Isn't that so?"

"Yes Ma'am. I meant no harm." Then, feeling bolder, he added, "I thought it'd be different here in Canada."

"You're right of course!" she replied and she showed nice teeth as she smiled at him underneath her stern black bonnet. "Don't be scared. I enjoy teasing a bit. That's my fun in life and today you gave me a gift."

"Oh," Seamus muttered, hanging his head down and wondering what she meant. All he could see now was a big black skirt with tiny black boots peaking out.

Now the voice was more commanding. "Look at me boy." Seamus lifted his head up. "Good. I think you were with young Josh when he came. Am I right?"

"Yes Ma'am."

"I thought so. I still have good eyes and I watched you two talking by this very bank. I'll let you catch some more fish on condition you tell me your name and play me another tune."

Seamus looked right into her sharp blue eyes and smiled awkwardly.

"I'm Seamus Maloney from out of Cork. What'd like to hear?" The lady replied in a thick Irish accent, "Now, be sure to play me that tune you were trying out. It's The Gentle Harpe if I remember rightly."

Seamus was taken aback and nearly stumbled over his rod. She continued, "I surprised you now, didn't I? Well my father was Robert

---

[1] A Gentle Harpe was the old name for the tune, Danny Boy.

Donovan a true man of Ireland so I heard the songs many a time. Play that one now, Seamus Maloney and then you can fish again." Seamus put the whistle to his mouth and smiled before he started to play the lovely melody. As he finished, the lady and her silent younger friend turned away with her words. "Maybe we'll see you another time," she said.

Seamus had never met with such kindness from a lady. He turned back to renew his line, encouraged by her words. After fishing steadily for an hour or so, he was thrilled to catch five whitefish big enough for supper.[2]

A typical school house built in the mid 19th century. The Dougall school house was built on the dock alongside James Dougall's store and a tinsmith's work place.

---
[2] Whitefish were plentiful at that time.

Chapter 7

Josh at the Dougall School

Josh usually enjoyed the last days at school before they had a summer break but each day he dreaded facing Billy Warton and the Innes boys.

Tom Fry and John Gordon were there as well as Mr. Dougall's three children, the Askins and Duff boys.

They were good friends but he alone had to face the threats of the Warton gang. Even though he was nearly thirteen years old, Josh was small for his age.

Facing bigger, stronger boys was something he tried to avoid. He had to hurry through the rainy streets down Murray Street, then past the tinsmith's on Market Square and into school. Just as he thought he was safe, he tripped over a stick and fell onto the wet boards. He saw no one but he heard laughter. Brushing off his front, he walked through the door into the one room school.

It was a relief to see Mr. Peden at his desk He looked up, noted Josh's wet appearance and said, "I see the weather has got to you, Josiah. The stove is on. Go and dry yourself."

"Thank you, sir," Josh replied, putting his small bundle down on a bench.

By the stove, Henry Fry was also drying his back and murmured, "You look like you've taken a fall, Josh. You have to watch the slippery boards."

"It was more than that Tom. I fell over a long stick. Tell you later."

"Right, boys," said their teacher when the other children came in. "We will do some more geography. Duncan Innes, bring the big globe over here."

Mr. Peden pointed to Europe on the globe and asked, "Who can name an island in Europe?"

Robert Dougall put up his hand. Mr. Peden nodded at him. "It's Great Britain, sir."

"Correct, Robert. Now who can name the small island west of it? More people are emigrating from it."

Josh realised this clue fitted Seamus' story. He put up his hand.

"Is it Ireland, sir?"

"Yes it is. Now how did you come to be so sure of it?"

"I met a new boy who came from there."

"Right. Do any of you know why the Irish are leaving their country this year?"

David Innes put his hand up and said, "It's 'cause they know they're better off here."

"Well, that's one reason many people come. But why are so many coming now?"

Into the silence Mr. Peden explained, "They have very little food. The potatoes they rely on, are rotten. They are starving."

Josh put up his hand adding, "The boy I met said the English had taken their land away. They had nowhere to live." Behind his back the Innes boy was nudged by Billy Warton who scowled at Josh and whispered, "Teacher's pet's at it again."

"None of that whispering Warton! Yes. People paid their rent in grain and had nothing to live on. In a bad harvest, they lost their homes. Some good men have helped them make a new start here. We need to know their sufferings and help too."

After a pause, he added, "Right. Now who can tell me the name of another European country. Think of people in this town and the language they speak."

Billy stood up and blurted out, "Scotland."

"That's part of Great Britain, William, but of course we do sound different," the teacher replied and with a chuckle, he added in a broad

Scots dialect, "Ye ken tell alle men by the tongue they spake!" The boys laughed appreciating his little joke.

"Now here's a clue," he stated. "What language does Mr. Fortier speak?" This time, Henry Fry smiled and his hand shot up. Mr. Peden pointed to this happy black boy. "He speaks 'le francais' of Lower Canada. His ancestors came from France."

"Good answer. Now who knows another?"

"Mr. Schultz speaks German. Is it Germany?" John Gordon asked.

"Good try, John. Some new immigrants speak German and English because their parents did. It is important to know connections to Europe because we trade with Europe. Many of our best writers come from that old continent. Good. Today, we shall do some spelling of country names. Get your slates and chalk ready."

The morning continued as usual with a little mathematics. Josh enjoyed this as he was quick from all the practice in the store. He also noted that Duncan Innes was smart when he was adding too. He'd liked to have got to know him more. Part way through the day, Mr. James Dougall came in to see Mr. Peden who was his cousin; the boys and the two quiet girls were allowed a break.

Going to the outhouse, Josh saw Henry Fry surrounded by the same boys who had bullied him. Henry was tall and tough but could he handle three boys at a time? Josh felt afraid for him and clutched at his stomach; the thought of facing these bullies made him feel sick. He was just turning back when he heard Henry say, "We were invited to this school. I don't care where I learn but I will do just as well as you!"

"Good for you, Henry" came the strong voice of James Dougall whose two children stood along side their father. "I chose to build a school where my children could learn tolerance and value everyone. I do not want any boys bullied by you Billy or your friends. Now get back inside!"

Josh was relieved and heartened to hear Mr. Dougall stand up for fair play but he knew that it would just irritate the 'Warton Gang'. He'd survive by keeping out of their way. Perhaps it was cowardly but he preferred peace.

Mr. Peden ended the day by reading part of Mr. Dickens' book, Nicholas Nickelby. They all enjoyed this and listened intently as

Nicholas coped with the journey to Yorkshire on a bleak winter's day with five nervous little boys and the villainous Mr. Squeers.

As they were leaving, Mr. Peden called Josh to him, "I'm off to the church, Josh so I'll walk with you."

Had Mr. Peden heard about the argument Henry had with Billy Warton? Reluctantly, he said, "Thank you, sir," He was unhappy to be receiving special treatment from the teacher.

Chapter 8

Meetings after School

Seamus had such success fishing that he went back almost daily to catch fish for his family. He hadn't seen the lady again but, today, it came on to rain so he left after just catching three fish. He hurried along the road home. He could feel water oozing into his old boots even though he tried to avoid puddles.

Then he saw Josh walking with a well dressed man. Seamus didn't like to say anything until Josh did. "Afternoon Seamus. You been fishing?"

Seamus nodded and the man turned to Josh. "Is this a friend of yours, Josiah?"

"Yes sir. He's the new immigrant from Ireland I told you about."

Seamus looked up at a fair-headed man with the deep voice. Although he was just taller than Seamus, he looked important in his dark suit with a high white cravat round his neck.

"Have you known Josiah long?" the teacher asked.

"Going on for a month, I 'spose. But I call him Josh."

"I see you have a bold tongue in your head! What's your name?"

"Seamus Maloney."

"Right! I'm Robert Peden. I hear your people have had a hard time with the potato blight."

"They have indeed, sir. Hard it was before we came." Seeing the teacher's interest, Seamus added boldly, "We'd nought to eat let alone pay a rent to the English landlord. We had to leave!"

"I can understand your anger, son. The Scots have had their problems with the English too. Like you I came here to have a be# er life and more freedom to help others. We all need to improve our chances."

As Mr. Peden finished, he eyed Seamus carefully. Josh saw his chance to ask what was on his mind now. "Sir, could I borrow some books to read with Seamus. He didn't have much time in school in Ireland."

Seamus looked up, surprised to hear Josh ask for help for him with reading. With a smile, Mr. Peden said, "Of course. Why not? I can advise you as well and Seamus will be reading all kinds of books in no time."

Seamus' face had coloured by this talk but, inside, he felt a new hope that he had not had for a long time. He looked up and said quietly, "And I'll be that glad to learn, sir."

"Good. Now I must go to the church. Goodbye to you both."

Seamus touched his cap and murmured, "Thanks, sir."

With that, Mr. Peden left, head bent against the fresh wind. His concerned look showed his desire to help. "He's a fine man, a minister at the Presbyterian Church and secretary of the Literary, Philosophical and Agricultural Society. I admire him," Josh said to Seamus. "He will stand by his word."

"Yes, I see. But Josh, do you know what goes on at the docks?"

"All kinds of things. Come on. We can look round together!" Seamus thought and asked, "I should be getting back. It won't take long, will it?"

They walked along together, noting all the different boats. The Parks' schooner was sailing out for Montreal past a small fishing boat. Josh spied David Innes watching the boats and plucked up the courage to speak to him alone.

"Hello, you enjoy watching the boats too?"

David turned and replied, "Yes, 'specially the new steamers. They're off to Buffalo. See that one coming in? I watched her being built at this yard."

"What's it called?" Josh asked.

"She's the Earl Cathcart, new this Spring," David Innes volunteered.

"I want to be a mariner one day."

"I came on a boat as big as that from Ireland," added Seamus.

"I expect they stuffed you in like sardines! You couldn't pay for the trip anyway!"

"Don't you talk about us Irish like that," answered Seamus. "Stick 'em up," he said getting ready to fight. "We're two to one of you now for a change."

Josh felt embarrassed and shuffled his feet in the dirt, "Don't Seamus. No need to make trouble!"

"What do I care," David Innes mumbled. "I'm far bigger than you anyway!" And, before Josh could stop them, they were hitting each other hard.

Seamus was down on the ground when Josh felt so angry that he tripped David Innes up. He was trying to pull Seamus to his feet when Mr. Park came over.

"What is going on here? Two boys attacking David! I'll have none of it. Be off with you before I tan your hides! You should be ashamed of yourselves." Then, Mr Park turned to David, "Are you all right ? Take yourself off home and I'll make sure these two ruffians don't bother you again."

By now, Josh, picking up his school books, knew he was late for his job at the store and Seamus, the worse for wear, had dropped his fish onto the dock. Both boys tried to wash them up quickly as Mr. Park supervised them. "Get right home now and don't be coming round my dock again until you improve your attitudes!"

Disheartened and humbled the two walked off quickly and silently until they mumbled, "See you." Then they parted. Josh was in a hurry but, as he went to cross the road, he just missed a cart.

"Watch out for my cart!" shouted an angry man, shaking his fist at Josh." I might 'o guessed. You coloureds don't even know how to walk down the street proper!"

Behind him, Josh heard someone laugh. He hung his head feeling tears come. He'd had enough for one day and part of it was his own fault. Within minutes he was back at the corner store where his uncle was standing in the doorway.

"Where have you been, boy? You due some fifteen minutes back!" His uncle said, looking angry. "Jobs need to be done and you go off when you be needed here."

"Yes sir," mumbled Josh, keeping his eyes down.

"Well, you shouldn't have dallied! Mr. Robert Elliott wants this message over to his house 'soon as possible. I can't leave the store. Those Elliotts have been good to us coloured folk. Least we can do is get a job done on time! Get to the Elliotts with this now and no shilly-shallying!"

"Yes sir," Josh replied and turned to go with the letter.

"No more stopping on the way. You hear me boy?" his uncle insisted.

Josh nodded and left at a good sprint. In no time he was panting his way past the tannery and the mill to get to the Elliott's back door quickly. He had to do his best. He bent down to relieve the ache in his side, thinking his uncle rarely sounded angry.

"Come in Josh," Sadie said, beckoning him through the door. "You be all out of breath. Here, have some water." she insisted, bringing him a cup while she talked. "Now what's this?"

"An important message from Master Elliott, Sadie. He needs something quick."

"I'll take it to the mistress now. She'd likely know." Sadie le# the kitchen. Josh heard her small quick steps and the rustle of skirts in the hallway. He was surprised when old Mrs. Elliott quietly came into the kitchen.

"I saw you run in, Josh," she started, "I met your young friend the other day. He plays the tin whistle well. Bring him over with you next time my grandchildren are visiting."

"Yes Ma'am. I didn't know he played."

"Oh didn't you, now?" Mrs. Elliott remarked. Her sharp old eyes didn't miss much. "He's good. I'd have him come for Francois' birthday soon. Come one afternoon when you're out of school."

"Yes of course, ma'am," Josh replied, hoping Seamus would be polite. Mrs. Elliott left as quietly as she'd come. Josh watched her neat round figure move off with her wide black skirt brushing past Sadie who was returning with a bigger package.

"Here, Josh. Missus Alice says to give the master this right away for the special meeting."

"Where'll I find him?" Josh asked.

"In the town council meeting at merchant Taylor's place today."

"Right. I'll do it straight away. Thanks for the water."

"No trouble Josh. I'll see ya."

With that Josh set out at a good stride for town, determined to fulfil his job well.

He did not want to be late for Mister Elliott's important meeting so he moved quickly across the street, tripping over some ruts in the road. He barely kept upright. As he tried to keep his balance he heard the mean high-pitched laughter out the side of a log home. He was sure it was Billy. This kind of jeering set his teeth on edge but he made it to the meeting place.

Mr. Barclay Elliott, who was the town's treasurer, saw him. "Ah, good," he said in a hearty voice. "You're just in time with the papers, I need. Here, Josh," he added taking a coin from his pocket. "Thank you."

"Thank you, sir," said Josh, looking at the shiny three-penny piece in his hand. "Glad to help." Then Josh left and returned to the store, feeling his luck had changed. He was delighted with this bonus.

Below is a picture of Dr. Park's house as it is today. Dr. Park was a relative of Mr. Park the merchant.

This may have been a bit like the inside of Seamus' family's home. They would not have had much furniture.

Chapter 9

Seamus' Lucky Day

Seamus had also hurried back home with Dermot on his shoulders down Richmond Street. He didn't enjoy walking with such a little one for long even if it helped his mother.

"Mam," he enthused. "Was there enough fish for supper?"

"It'll do us fine. I've made bread," his mother said sounding more cheerful. "Your Da loves any fresh fish on his plate. Now, you'll be after going down to the stables and telling your Da Mr. Maloney wants to see him. It may bring him home for supper sooner."

"I will indeed Mam. That'll be the man who talked to me at the well," Seamus added.

Seamus almost skipped to the stables to give his father the news.

He wondered, 'Would it mean a better place to live? Anything would be an improvement!' He found his father busy brushing down a big old brown horse. "Hello Da. It's me. I've news."

Patrick Maloney a wiry little man, turned around smiling. He tousled the boy's brown hair. "Well, this is a fair treat, a visitor from my own family!" he exclaimed. "What's the big news?"

"Ma wants you to come early to see Mr. Maloney," Seamus said, smiling all over his face. "And Da, I caught our supper again; it's whitefish."

"Well done, my boy. I've a bit to finish up here. Play me Piping Tim and I'll work more quickly."

Seamus took out his whistle, playing such a merry tune that his father whistled to it.

"That's done now!" pronounced his father patting the horse before he put away the saddle.

As Seamus continued to play, he noticed two men by the barn door, listening. One was tapping his foot a bit. "That's a fine tune your boy plays, Patrick. He's real good. Mrs. Drake ought to hear him. They'd be glad of a tune come nightfall at the inn."

Seamus stopped and heard the other man say, "Pity we didn't have him round this past winter but we have special days in June. Many Frenchies round here like a bit of music on St. Jean's day. You play for Mrs. Drake, boy." He finished pointing at Seamus and then, beckoning with his hand, he suggested, "Why not go over there now?"

"Thank you, sir but we have to go home."

"It'll only take a few minutes. Come with me. I'm Thomas Paxton," he said offering a friendly hand to Seamus. "Follow me." Seamus looked back at his father.

"Go ahead boy. I'll find you soon. We won't be late for your Mam." Seamus entered the side door of the big hotel, passing by a small room into a larger open area which was full of men chatting. In one corner, he saw an older lady dressed in a shiny brown skirt with a bright stripped top. Her sharp green eyes looked at him over her broad folded arms.

"Evening, Ann," said Mr. Paxton. "Have I got a treat for you!"

"Well, I certainly need it tonight. What is it?"

"Here. See this boy? He plays the tin whistle. Go on son. Play!" Seamus was feeling a bit shy in this big place and he started up poorly but the soothing melody of The Gentle Harpe took over as he closed his eyes and remembered what his grandfather had taught him. He wasn't immediately aware that the conversation round him stopped and everyone was listening. When he finished the tune, Mrs. Drake just looked directly at him.

"That's a great job you did with a lovely old tune. Just imagine what we'd do if we added a fiddle and a singer. What's your name, boy?"

"Seamus Maloney, ma'am," he replied, his eyes on the dusty floor.

An Unexpected Friendship

"Oh, you'll be Patrick's son with a tongue like that!" she commented.

"How about coming here on a Friday and Saturday for an hour and giving us some more tunes. I'll pay you according to how all my people enjoy it. What do you say?"

"I'll have to ask . . ." Seamus voice trailed off.

But he heard his father state, "Of course he'll come! He'll brighten your night to be sure and all."

"Then we'll see you in three days' time, Seamus," said Mrs. Drake.

Overwhelmed, all Seamus could say was, "Thank you, ma'am," before he left with his father. When they got home, Mary, little Dermot and his mother were waiting.

"We nearly gave up on you," his mother scolded. "Come now. Eat up. Seamus brought in fish."

"This has been a good day for you and all, Seamus," commented his father, adding, "Mary, the boy has a job playing at Searle's Inn an hour or two. Aye, he learned well from your father."

The children ate sitting on the straw on the floor while their parents used the only two chairs. But the meal was filling and before long his parents were relaxed, talking of old times. Mary smiled and little Dermot was marching around. Seamus realized that they were happy for the first time in ages! Just then, Mr. Maloney hollered in, "Can I come in? Need to see you."

"Of course, Mr. Maloney," said his mother, hurriedly collecting bowls and taking them off the table. "Now Mary and Seamus take Dermot out for a minute while we talk."

Seamus hung back, wanting to stay but, catching a hard look on his mother's face, all he said was, "Yes Mam," as he followed Mary out.

At the door, Mr. Maloney stopped him, smiling. "Oh Seamus, I heard about your playing at Searle's. That's great for sure. I'll be listening."

"Thank you," Seamus said, returning the smile. Outside, Mary wanted to skip with an old rope. Seamus tied the rope to an old post and turned the other end. He tried hard to hear the voices inside, leaning towards the house and just barely watching over Dermot.

It seemed an age before his father and Mr. Maloney came out, all smiles. They both looked at the children.

"It's a fine family you have there, Patrick," said Mr. Maloney. "I look forward to having you nearer me. My Michael's around your age, Seamus. He helps me on the farm."

"Thank you, Michael and the Lord bless you for your kindness this day," Seamus' father replied.

"I'll be saying goodbye to you till next week then. Let me know what help you need."

"I will that and thank you again," his father promised. Mr. Maloney had no sooner gone than Seamus blurted out, "What did he say, Da?"

"Oh, he's a good man, ready to help a fellow Irishman. He's offered us a cabin on his land and he'll sell us ten acres if we clear them ourselves. Now what do you think of that?"

"That's wonderful, Da! To be sure, it will be better for us all. When can we move?"

"Well, you heard him, my boy. It will be on a day I can get away from the stables next week; usually a Tuesday's slow but I'll see," his father informed him.

We can go to a proper house, Da, can we?" asked Mary jumping up and down.

Her father picked her up, twirled her around and laughed. Seamus was happy and went in to see his mother.

He found her resting her head on the table, her eyes closed. Was she so tired that her response to the good news was to rest? Or was she ill? Seamus looked at the lines around her eyes and mouth; she looked older than her thirty-six years. Perhaps that was why his father stayed out with the two youngsters. Seamus wanted to put his arms round her. She deserved a nice place. All her energy seemed to be used up.

She'd heard his step and said, "Oh Seamus, I must have nodded off. It's great news, we have now. Isn't it?"

"Yes, it is Mam. Can I go tell my new friend, Josh, now?" Seamus Asked.

"Not now, Seamus. I seem fair worn out tonight. Our Dermot wears me out!"

"Then, rest yourself now, Mam. Da and I will see to the little ones."

Chapter 10

Josh visits His Family

Josh was glad to finish school by the Thursday before Easter. No more early morning walks, no bullies around as Billy was kept busy in summer by his father. Josh looked forward to seeing his parents who were clearing land out of town in the new settlement in Colchester. After the store had been closed, his aunt waved him goodbye and gave him a bundle of cheese and fresh butter for his mother. "Now we'll look for you all at the church come Sunday," she said.

Josh felt proud to be taking good food with him, knowing his mother had little time to churn butter. It was a clear evening for a long walk and on the way, he picked some fiddleheads in the ditches. He followed the Colchester road out to the third concession spot and three hours later, he was being hugged by his own mother. It felt so good!

"My, my do you look grand, Josh. It's so good to have you with us in. You'll have to read to us tonight."

"Course, Mama, I'll read what you like. I've learned so much with Mr. Peden. But I've missed your stories."

"Oh go on with you. I'll be forgetting those times now. You go find your Dada out back."

Josh was surprised to see his father had chopped down many trees around the house that winter. With some logs, he'd built a small barn big enough for their one cow, two pigs and a few chickens.

"It looks real good, Dada," Josh said.

"So do you, son," his father replied. Then he teased, "You even have some muscles on you now! You be ready to do all my work soon."

"Don't think so, Dada but I am sure ready to help. I also heard how you and Uncle Jim helped stop the Rebels when I was little. You never told me 'bout that, Dada!"

"That was just one day's job, boy. But it got us our land, right enough. But you come and tell me 'bout all your learnin'. That's what I need to know."

Josh walked back into the strong log cabin again. Soon his two sisters were clinging to him, tugging on his pockets.

"Have you brought me anything?" Angelina asked.

"Oh, I forgot," he teased. But when she looked downcast, he pulled out two coloured ribbons. "Here you are. You can choose which you want. Who likes the pink?"

"I do!" said his dainty five year old sister, Corrie.

"You can have it, I like the blue one," the nine tear old Angelina stated primly. "Thank you, Josh."

"What's your news, son?" Josh's mother asked. "Tell us. Have you seen Sadie?"

"Sadie sends her best to you. Hopes to see you at the church come one Sunday. She's fine. Uncle Jim keeps me busy and I read when Mr. Peden lends me books."

"That's good son. You keep it up. We may need a school here one day for our new settlers. We'll need someone like you."

"What you mean, Dada? I want to stay in school another year or two. There's much more to learn."

"Now, don't think we be rushing it. I be meanin' a school for our own kind, son where no one bothers us. Enough free people coming in here and to Gilgal that we needs us our own school."

"Don't you get along with the white folk here, Dada?"

"Course we do. Just that we sees the needs to come. We'll show what we can do with learnin' with a teacher of our own."

"Now, you stop that talk, Peter Stokes, right this minute and let us all sit to eat my stew. Our boy's walked a long way tonight."

"Not as long as you once did Mama," Josh said quietly, smiling at her.

His father went back outside with Josh, splashed his face and hands in the rain tub, dried them on the nearby cloth and, putting his arm round Josh, he said, "Let's eat what your Mama has made us and give God above our thanks."

After supper was cleaned up, Josh watched his mother drop into a strong arm chair, his father had made. She took a deep breath, closed her eyes for a moment and then smiled at him. "Come and sit here Josh. It'll be like old times again. I 'member what a good baby you was for me. You loved music. Member that special song that gave us the spirit to come north?"

"You mean 'Swing Low Sweet Chariot', coming for to carry us home?"

"That's one of them. T' other was this that we'd hear," his mother replied and started to sing in her lovely strong voice,

> "Go down Moses,
> 'Way down in Egypt land
> Tell ol' Pharaoh
> To let my people go."

Soon she'd inspired them all to sing with her.

At the end, Angelina asked, "Why did that help you Mama?"

"Well, Angelina, we knew God never meant us to be slaves. He wanted us all to be free so the song helped us to make up our minds and follow the north star. You've heard the story before."

"I know but I love to hear how you got away and how people helped you, Dada and baby Josh," Angelina said as she poked Josh in the ribs.

"It's still fresh in my memory though it's over ten years since we found freedom. We be lucky cause your Dada knew the woods and rivers round that old Kentucky plantation. We saved us corn meal cakes and left on a new moon night. Your Dada knew of an old rowboat and we used it to reach way down river. Early next morning we hid amongst trees near the swamps while we heard the master's dogs barking. But they couldn't get us! We moved on again at night. Just as I was getting real tired, we found us a barn to sleep in. Then next mornin' a man in a big hat came in and heard Josh's crying."

"What happened then, Mama?" Corrie asked.

Their mother smiled broadly. "That was the best thing to happen although we be scared first. The man was a Quaker man who couldn't 'bide slavery. He fed us, gave us clothes and took us on to the next station on the underground railroad."

"That's a wonderful thing, they do," interrupted their father. "They save so many of us and show us ways to get to Canada. Why some men on this 'railroad' are free coloureds who never been slaves."

"That's true enough. It was one free man who took us in a covered wagon under his hay, one day. We heard him being questioned 'bout us but he never let on. We met some others in Ohio who were planning on coming to Canada through Detroit. They knew about the British fort at Malden so we joined with them. Couldn't have done it without all that help and lots of praying. I thank the good Lord every day for this free place."

"And that's why we are free, free, free!" exclaimed the joyful Angelina.

"And that's why Josh, you and Corrie can learn readin' and writin' now," their father added.

"How'd you know reading then, Dada?" asked Corrie.

"'Cause I listened when I heard the men talk about notices. I tried to follow some letters I saw on them cotton bales. I heard about a night school, a visitor gave, so I'd go after a long day on the field. I's glad I learned my letters. I was lucky I wasn't caught and walloped! The owners didn't like us having any learnin'. But this good man who came 'bout year 'fore we escaped, told me ABCs and some useful place names to know. He'd draw a map in the dirt and rub it out when we knowed it. He gave us hope. Now I made us some money, gonna send for your uncle Randolph."[3]

"How come you'll do that Dada?" asked Josh.

"Oh Reverend Bibb has his contacts in Detroit. They get the word out and down to Kentucky. I just gives some money. I know he'll come one day."

"Now, that's the end of the story telling for you all. No light left and plenty to do in the morning!" their mother said.

---

[3] Randolph Stokes arrived on the steamship Pearl in 1850

Josh's parents' cabin in the New Settlement (later called Harrow) may have looked like this.

Chapter 11

Seamus Fights Back

Seamus found it hard waiting to see Josh who was away for two days visiting his family. There was plenty to do to help his mother feel sure they could move their meagre belongings safely. His father came home with the good news that Mr. Fry was willing to loan him a horse and cart on the Tuesday morning as long as he could get the moving done quickly.

"Sure and he's a kind man, Marie. With Seamus here we should be able to take you and the children with your spinning wheel, the loom and pots first and come back for the other odds and ends," Seamus' father reassured his mother. It was good to see her smile.

Seamus took the chance to ask if she needed any goods to take with them. She did and his father also mumbled something about onion bulbs if the store had them before he set out for the stables again. "No loitering, mind you!" his mother commanded. "I need you back here soon."

"Right, Mam. But I know Josh will be interested in our news. Mr. Alexander offered to lend Da tools for clearing land." Seamus waved goodbye and headed for Alexander's Grocery Store.

He had gone just a small distance when he saw the Warton gang of three hanging around in front of the Meloche Building Yard. Billy was the first to shout out, "Come here, you Irish. Now listen up! It's not right for us whites to be friends with coloureds. Have you got that?"

Seamus turned away, trying to cross over to the other part of the street but Billy pushed in front of him. "Answer when you're spoked to, young 'un." He caught hold of Seamus' jacket.

"Let me go," Seamus told him, pushing Billy away with two hands, "I'll not let anyone waylay me! I'm older than you and Josh is my friend."

"Really," said Billy. "Maybe I should teach you a lesson. What you think, boys?"

"Go ahead, Billy. No teacher about here," chorused the Innes boys, waving their arms in the air . . .

Billy swiped at Seamus who ducked quickly. Seamus then gave him a punch in the stomach.

"Oh, that does it!" Billy exclaimed, hitting Seamus on the cheek.

"Got you this time!"

"Now, now, now," said Mr. Meloche, pushing the boys apart, "I'll have none of that around here." He was followed by Mr. Maloney who stared at Seamus.

"Seamus, I'm surprised at you fighting! We Irish don't want that kind of reputation."

"I'm just protecting myself, sir." Seamus said wiping a bloody cheek.

"And what about you, Billy?" asked Mr. Meloche.

"He hit me first!"

"Is that true, boys?" asked Mr. Maloney of the Innes boys. "And I want the truth out of you."

David Innes began, "He did Mr. Maloney. He wouldn't listen to Billy."

"He would'na listen at all," claimed Duncan.

"Is that true, Seamus?"

Seamus was angry and blurted out, "Billy is trying to stop me seeing Josh and I won't! It was himself who threatened me. He went to hit me, I ducked and caught him in the stomach. Then he hit me back."

"Well it didn't improve matters for either of you. Try to solve your problems other ways or stay apart. Do you hear me, boys?" Mr. Maloney demanded.

"If you don't see eye to eye, agree to differ. No more of that," Mr. Meloche advised.

The three bigger boys left and Seamus was stopped by Mr. Meloche.

"You'd better come and splash some cold water on that face before you leave. Where're you headed?"

"To Mr. Alexander's store to see Josh." While Seamus splashed the water on his face, he caught the two men's talk. Mr. Meloche said, "Now I see why he was stopped. Mixing don't work with some. I can see there'll be trouble afoot if we don't put an end to this back-biting, John. It's because James Dougall will have his school open to all. I've heard the talk round town. Peden's a good teacher. I don't mind the mixing but some don't abide it."

Seamus came out refreshed. "Thank you Mr. Meloche."

"You're welcome." With that he turned back to a piece of wood, one of many alongside his big boat building barn. Mr. Maloney, resting one food against the wood, stroked his chin.

"We used to get along with the coloureds here but I can see your point François. There's more coloureds coming in every day. Now I believe in freedom and can't abide slavery but we got to think of the future. It's time they had a good school of their own, I s'pose. I must be off. Good day to you." Then he added, "Watch yourself, Seamus!"

"Au revoir, mon ami. And Seamus, don't get into trouble again!" Mr. Meloche added with a grin.

Seamus had heard enough. What a problem Josh faced! What was wrong with being friends with someone of a different colour? Mr. Alexander was much kinder than any white Englishman had been. Whatever happened he was on Josh's side.

He was soon inside the store, asking Mr. Alexander for the few items of flour, butter and tea his mother wanted. Josh came in from the back as cheerful as ever. "Hi, Seamus. Did you practice any letters?"

"I did some, Josh but we got other things to do now. My da has got us a cabin and some land. We move tomorrow. Then I'll work at my letters."

"Oh that is good news," Mr. Alexander said. "Now remember you can borrow any tools to get started."

"I told Mam that. Thank you. Would you be having any onion bulbs? Da asked about them."

"I can spare you some. Usually you put aside your own. Is there anything else?"

"No thank you Mr. Alexander. But can I talk to Josh?" Josh's uncle nodded and went out to the back. "Josh, I had a bit of a fight with that Billy Warton. He was trying to stop me seeing you. I won't have any of it!"

"He's a real bully," Josh replied. "But he'll soon be busy working on his dad's land and now, you'll be out of his reach. I'd rather forget about him. Let's do some reading in the evenings. Mr. Peden has given me two books to read with you."

"I'd like that Josh. I think it will help me a lot. I must go now. Mam said she did not want me lingering." With that Seamus went off with his goods.

Chapter 12

Summer Jobs

During the busy late Spring and Summer days, Josh and Seamus managed to meet enough times for Seamus to feel more competent with his reading. He soon remembered all his letters and could write simple useful words down. Josh encouraged him to learn how to spell words like tea, butter, cheese, flour and potatoes that he needed for his mother's lists, and place names round the town.

During the summer of 1846, the boys both grew quite a bit. Seamus felt stronger and more confident from all the farm work he did with Mr. Maloney and his own father. He helped to clear trees, chop wood and plant vegetables. Most of all he liked learning to plough behind Mr. Maloney's strong oxen. He enjoyed mastering the skill of trying to plough a straight furrow and laughed shyly when Mr. Maloney said, "You're getting the hang of it now Seamus. You'll be a farmer yet!"

Josh still gave his uncle time at the store but, for two weeks in late May and all June, he worked alongside his father, planting his corn and tobacco crops as well as helping mother with the kitchen vegetable garden. In the evening he would read to the family or go fishing with his father in the nearby creeks. It was then that his father again emphasised the need to educate himself well. "You'll get on with learnin' Josh. You be a patient boy. I sees you a teacher and a help to us all. When God helped me get free, I told him I'd see you become a real learner. I'm proud of you son!"

"Thank you Dada. I like to learn and my friend Seamus is learning from me."

"Good for you, Josh. We can do right well with good learnin'. You know that friend of mine, George McCoy? He's thinking of moving out of here to get his children a better education. His Elijah is so curious his dada says he's asking him questions all the day long!

Yep, he's real sharp that one and he only be 'bout six. He 'minds me of you at the same age, Josh."

"So you've told me afore!" Josh replied, as he pulled up a small fish. "But I do like to be with all the family out here. How's Mr. Matthews now?"

"Fine and all his six children. His cabin be down on this third road, just east of us. Mighty fine farmer he is too. We get along fine." After a pause Josh's father said, "Let's head back home now son and see if we can make something of our catch."

Later that day, Josh asked to go to see Seamus at the store. "I'll stay over a night or two, Mama. See if Uncle Jim has any need of help. He'll be using his grandson John who isn't so used to the work as me."

"That's fine Josh," his mother replied. "You can bring me some necessities and deliver this bit of quilting to Sadie on your way in."

Josh left at a good pace, glad that the daylight lasted longer now. As he got onto the Colchester Road towards Amherstburg, he saw a cart drawn by a nice brown horse coming along. Soon he recognised Mrs. Elliott's grand children with their father. He waved, expecting them to go on but they stopped.

"Evening Reverend," Josh said politely, tipping his large brimmed straw hat.

"Would you like a ride into town, Josiah?" Rev. Francis Elliott asked as he stopped his horse.

"Thank you, sir."

"Then jump on the back by our Francis."

Josh felt a sudden pull and soon had the joy of the ride to Rev. Elliott's mother's house on the outskirts of Amherstburg.

"We're going to visit grandmother," one little girl said eagerly.

"That's nice," Josh commented. "She's a real kind lady. I've often gone there to deliver goods."

"That's where we met you before," said Francis. "Grandmother says you have a friend who plays an Irish whistle well. What's his name?"

"That would be Seamus Maloney. I hope to see him tomorrow."

"Can you bring him over to the house when we are there?" Francis asked. "We are staying with grandmother for two days."

"I can try," replied Josh. "If I get hold of him tomorrow, we could come in the evening."

"Right-on! That would be a change, wouldn't it Alice?" Francis said turning to his sister.

"Yes. I'd like that, Josh," Alice added quietly.

They reached the Elliott house and Josh got down off the cart before the family headed up the long drive.

"Thank you, sir. Bye Francis and Alice," Josh called as he waved goodbye. Now he'd have to find Seamus. He'd give Sadie the quilting another day.

At about the same time, Seamus was off playing at Searle's Inn. He was now quite at ease there and enjoyed playing for the guests for an hour or so. He was always paid promptly by Mrs. Drake and offered a hearty snack. Tonight it was hot so he played on the doorstep for the people who chose to drink outside on the wooden porch. He'd played a couple of jigs, a love song and a French folk song he'd picked up during the summer. Then Mr. Maloney asked him to play one of Ireland's haunting old tunes. He chose The Gentle Harpe and soon heard Mr. Maloney humming the tune as well as putting in words he could remember.

"Tis a fine old melody, that is," Mr. Maloney said as Seamus put his whistle down. "Sure you soothe the hearts of us all to hear it. Thank you Seamus."

Seamus nodded and was offered an apple cider to drink. It was lovely and cool after all the playing. Soon he got away to see if his father was finished in the stables. He found him putting in new straw while a man held his horse. "Will you give him a brush down and his food, Patrick?" asked the man.

"Sure I will. I still have to feed the other horses," Seamus' father answered. Then he said, "Ah, Seamus me boy, give me a tune while I work."

"I will that Da." Then, taking out his whistle, he played a happy jig. Afterwards he asked, "Da, can I go down by the river and see if any fish are jumping? Sometimes I have luck at night."

"You do that Seamus. Here's my rod. I fancy a bit of fish for supper."

"Thanks Da. Shall I come back here?"

"No, just head up home on Murray and I may catch you up. I'm using Mrs. Drake's horse and cart tonight to bring your mother a treat. It's in those two sacks. See."

Seamus looked to see the sacks brim full of sheep's wool. "Mam will be pleased Da! She loves to weave."

"And right good at it she is," his father replied. "Now, away with you and don't be bothering me any more or I'll change me mind," he added with a laugh.

The Elliott House was built of brick around 1835 in Amherstburg. It was in a Georgian style—rather square with nice big windows. It may have had a balcony at one time but does not have one now. Note the chimneys at either end. Below is a picture of how it looks today.

Chapter 13

More Developments

Seamus was happily sitting on the river bank catching some white fish when Josh came by. "This is wonderful," Josh said enthusiastically. "I thought I'd have to look for you, Seamus."

"Good to see you Josh. What do you want? Have you any new books for me, yet?"

"None till I ask Mr. Peden, Seamus. But I'm glad you've covered the early reader."

"Yes. I read it to Mary and she liked the stories too. My mother is real proud of my reading now," Seamus replied. "Our Mary wants me to teach her letters too but there's not much time. I work on our land, help Mr. Maloney and tonight I've been playing at Searle's."

"That's why I wanted you. Remember old Mrs. Elliott? Her grand children know about you and want to hear you play. They are just here for two days. Could you play for them tomorrow afternoon? I could let Sadie know to tell them."

"I might be able to get away an hour before I go to Searle's this Friday. That'd be 'bout six of the clock. I know my Mam would want me to play for Mrs. Elliott as I told her she liked my playing a while back."

"Then, that settles it. I was just into the store and Sadie is visiting so I'll tell her the good news. Must go now." But Josh added, "I'll get another book tomorrow. Let's meet at the Park's wharf."

"I'll be there," Seamus replied as he picked up his rod and four small fish to head home up Murray Street.

The next day, Seamus worked hoeing round his family's vegetables with his mother. Again he noticed how tired she was but she would be, he thought, with another babe coming soon. It was hot for her and she was constantly checking on Dermot and Mary playing nearby. After an hour she called to Mary to bring water and told Seamus,

"I'll be going in to see to food. Finish up and bring the children in." Seamus nodded and went on with the work. Mary brought up a cool drink which he swallowed gratefully.

Seamus thought how hot summer days were here and hard to work in; it was much hotter than Ireland. But it was good to be here and he always had enough to eat. His mother still seemed to have days when she could not cope although their two roomed cabin was always clean and his father had managed to buy his mother some bright cloth for curtains at the window as well as sheep's wool to spin. When the sun was high in the sky, Seamus called, "Let's go in, you two. Mam will be ready for us now. Wash at the tub as you go in, remember."

Mary and Dermot soon left their simple game played with a small wheel and stick at the edge on the field. It was forever falling over the lumpy clay soil but they enjoyed the play. Once their meal of bread, cheese and some new beans were eaten, Seamus told his mother about the Elliott's request to play.

"They just want to hear a bit of Irish music," he said, trying to persuade his mother to let him go. "I can still get plenty done today."

"You shall go Seamus," agreed his mother. "I want you to choose the right moment and ask a favour for me. I'm that anxious to contact my Harte family back home and the Elliotts will know how to go about getting a letter out. We have the money saved now to bring your Aunt Catherine and her family here. I'm worried about them all."

So that was why his mother looked far away sometimes. "Of course, I'll ask, Mam. I think Mrs. Elliott will help. Her son is the town treasurer; he'd know."

Some hours later Seamus strode down the road towards the river front where he had arranged to meet Josh, determined to use the opportunity to help his mother.

"Hello there, Seamus. I saw Mr. Peden today. I have a book for you. It even has some poems," Josh announced.

"That's good Josh. Can you hear me read? I'd like to try the new book."

With that the two boys sat down on the wooden planks by the river. Stacks of wood were ready for the frequent steamers that came into Amherstburg from Detroit or Buffalo. Nearby men were still working unloading a schooner for the Park merchants. There was always plenty to see. Any other day, that's just what Seamus would have done but he was keen to improve his reading now.

"Here's a poem I love," said Josh. "We learned it at school. It's by Mr. William Wordsworth. It's about a rainbow and I like them." Seamus began reading slowly and deliberately. "'My heart leaps up when I behold a rainbow in the sky. So was it when my life began; so is it now I am a man or else I die.' That's an odd thing to say!" Seamus added. "But I do like rainbows."

"It gets even deeper. This man was a real thinker, Mr. Peden says, as he talks of the child being 'father to the man'. I had to think about that a long time. Read it again, then we must go or we'll be late. Sadie told me that the children came for one of Mr. Robert's children's birthday. That's why they wanted the music."

The boys were soon racing past the elms at Elliott's Point to the big brick house.

"Come in Josh," welcomed Sadie. "So this is your friend Seamus! Welcome. The mistress is a-waiting you coming for the children. I think they'd like to hear music and have a game with it from all I hear."

Sadie led the way through to the front room. It was the grandest room either of the boys had ever seen. The floor had polished wood planks and on it was one fancy rug near the big open fireplace now unlit. Near one wall was a fine table and a fancy settle covered in a kind of gold brocade. Mrs. Elliott sat in another easy chair by the mantle, watching her grandchildren examine a small toy castle on the floor. Mr. Robert and his wife Mrs. Alice Elliott were all smiles as they greeted the boys who felt shy.

"Ah, the music man!" said Mr. Robert with a hearty smile. "Good to see you too Josh. Now mother what shall he play?"

"I'll have 'The Gentle Harpe' first and the children can have their music after," she answered. Then, looking at the children, she added,

"Now listen children. This boy can play a tune my grandfather played for me."

Seamus took out his whistle and was soon playing the lovely melody Mrs. Elliott knew so well. After that, when Mrs. Elliott nodded, he went into a jig. The children loved it responding by springing to their feet.

"Seamus, your music is so catchy that it makes me want to dance," said Mrs. Alice Elliott. "You play well. Our son would like to play a game. Can you play, stopping at any time and the children will find a seat to sit on? It's an old family game, musical chairs."

"I will that," said Seamus, anxious to oblige. Josh looked on, beaming at the fun the Elliott children had.

After the game, Mr. Robert said, "Sadie tells me you sing Josh. How about a tune for us now?"

"I'm not that good but I love singing 'Swing low, Sweet Chariot.' Will that suit, sir?"

"I heard that years ago when we first helped the freed slaves. What voices they had! Sing on Josh."

Josh began rather quietly but then he closed his eyes, thought of his family and sang out the melody he knew so well. As he finished,

"Swing low, sweet chariot, comin' for to carry me home," he opened his eyes and saw small Alice watching him with tears in her eyes.

"That was lovely, Josh I never knew you sung so well." Mrs. Alice Elliott said." I'm going to tell Mr. Peden we should have you two for one of our concerts."

"Thank you Missus Elliott. I just like to sing sometime—like Seamus here plays."

"You make a good pair. Thank you. Now go along to Sadie and she'll give you a special bun and a drink each."

"Thank you, Missus," Seamus said. Then he looked up and asked boldly, "Mr. Elliott, sir, could you help my mother get a message to Ireland, please?"

He'd done it! He asked what his mother needed to know and soon he heard the reply. "You tell your mother to write the letter and I will see it is franked to go on to Montreal and across the sea. Does she want her family to come here?"

"Yes, sir, she does. She is often lonely for them. My Aunt Catherine, Uncle Joseph and their children would be better off here too. I know it."

"You're right, Seamus. Bring me the letter and I'll see what I can do for you. It will take some months to reach Ireland but they'll get it."

"Thank you, sir. I'll be going now to my job at Searle's. It was good to play for you, Ma'am," he finished turning to old Mrs. Elliott who smiled and winked at him.

Sadie gave the boys a currant bun each and some apple cider before they left.

"That was fun!" Josh exclaimed." We should try to do some songs together."

"I'd like that but I must hurry so I'm not late. It's almost time for Searle's. Bye."

"Goodbye Seamus. Don't forget your reading.

Chapter 14

Exciting news for Seamus

Seamus continued to improve his reading as the summer months went by. He'd had the letter sent to his relatives, the Harte family and he felt more confident and happier in himself as he played with small Mary and Dermot. His mother was easily exhausted as her baby was due in six months. She rested more away from the extreme heat, Malden was having in August 1846. Her main interest seemed to be in Dermot now 3 years old; she left hoeing to Seamus who tended the small vegetable patch close by the house. As he hoed, he felt proud of his growing muscles as much as his ability to read and play his music. He felt more grown up! Soon he would be 15 years old and he was old enough to do a man's job. He wondered about going to sea as his grandfather had told him many tales.

Just as he was dreaming of what he might do, Mr. Maloney came up and patted him on the back, "Seamus, my boy, I've been thinking that you and my Michael John could go into the new ploughing competition come this Fall. Some of us in the Agricultural Society were thinking of having an Agricultural Show where we'd bring our best livestock and show off our good wheat, oats and corn. You boys can try your hand at the plough and the ladies will bake treats for us all. It'll be a grand time! Would you try it?"

"Do you think I'm good enough?" Seamus asked.

"Of course. You'll be in the boys' group. No need to worry and we'll have some practices when we've taken off the corn."

"Right; then. I'll try," Seamus replied beaming. Life was looking good.

Two months later in the cooler Fall weather and after much practice, Michael John and Seamus entered the ploughing match down on an empty field near the town. Around them, people congregated, talking happily and Seamus noticed Josh with three adults and two little girls he did not know. He waved before going over to find out when his turn came. He was glad Josh was watching.

Michael John was amongst the first to go along with Billy Warton. They both did well. Michael was very strong for a twelve year old. Both boys ploughed nice straight furrows. Seamus had to admit that Billy was good at it.

Then he heard his name announced and another boy he did not Know, by the name of John Wright. They went to another part of the field and got ready to plough it back to the centre.

The land was hard and dry as there'd been little rain. He knew he'd have to keep the horse steady as she walked into the field where bits of corn stalks still stood. Once they started Seamus concentrated on the furrow and the horse in front of him but he finished after the Wright boy.

"You did a good job," his father said. "Pity your mam isn't here yet."

"Thanks, Da. I enjoyed trying but I know the other boys are better."

The match went on with four other boys trying their hand at it. In the end Michael came in second and got a little money to spend. Seamus just enjoyed himself. As he and his father turned round, they both saw Mr. Elliott coming towards them with a package in his hand.

"Ah, Mr. Maloney. I'm pleased to give you this letter from Ireland. It was sent to me as I'd franked the one you sent. Good news I hope."

"Thank you Mr. Elliott. What do I owe you for the letter?" Seamus' father asked.

"Think nothing of it, sir. Seamus can pay us with a tune or two later. May I know if your news is good?"

An Unexpected Friendship

"Of course." Then Patrick Maloney opened the letter and read the fine print. Seamus looked on, hopeful of good news. Soon he heard his father say excitedly, "They're coming! They were to leave Cork on a boat called the John Francis. Catherine, who's been sick wrote this before they left. She is cheered by hopes of coming here. Oh, thank you so much, Mr. Elliott. This is good news indeed."

"I'm so pleased for you. I'll bid you good day then," said Mr. Elliott, tipping his hat with a smile. "I will look up the sailing lists in the Montreal paper when it arrives. Seamus you can come and find out."

"Thank you, sir. He will," Patrick Maloney replied.

Seamus couldn't hold his excitement! "Mam will be so pleased. Can I run and tell her when she comes?"

"She should be here shortly with Mrs. Maloney and our little ones. I know John went to fetch them in his wagon after he unloaded the wheat.

In a short while Seamus watched his mother arrive in the wagon seated next to Mrs. Maloney. She looked happy and he was glad to be giving her good news.

"Mam, we've good news from Aunt Catherine. They're on their way!"

Seamus mother who was being helped off the wagon by his father, almost fell into his arms! "Oh I can hardly believe it! News of my Harte family at last. Do you know the boat they're on?"

"Yes. It's the John Francis," Patrick replied, "And Mr. Elliott will find out when it arrives for us."

"That's splendid news indeed!" exclaimed Mrs. Maloney "Now, let's take our fresh cheeses to the table." The two ladies hurried off chatting happily and Seamus found Mary and Dermot jumping up and down at his heels. This was going to be a day to remember what with a picnic as well. Seamus watched his mother smiling for once.

But a week later Mr. Elliott came to Seamus' father at Searle's with a new problem. "Good day to you, Mr. Elliott," said Patrick Maloney.

"Good day. I have some news for you about the immigrants from Ireland," Mr. Charles Elliott replied looking very serious. "I read the Montreal paper and many boats coming from Ireland and Liverpool have immigrants in very poor health The officials are worried about

—
63

disease Some have had typhus and have died at sea so there is a place where they quarantine the people for a while. There is no knowing who is kept back. I just want you to be prepared Mr. Maloney." Patrick Maloney looked up, his face grave. His wife had put so much store by having her sister with her for the new baby's birth.

"I thank you, sir. I will try to prepare my wife."

"Now there's good news too. The Hartes were possibly on a better steamer and, since they had some money, they would have got some provisions for the journey. Their letter was dated late September 1846 and it is now October 18th. They may have landed and don't know how to get word to you," suggested Mr. Elliott. "Give me their names Mr. Maloney; we can put an advertisement into the paper."

"That is more than kind of you, sir. I will pay for placing the advertisement. They are Joseph and Catherine Harte with three daughters Winifred, Catherine and Elizabeth aged about 17, 15 and 13, I believe."

"That will do," said Mr. Elliott in a business like tone. "I'll let you know when I hear anything. It may take a few weeks."

"Thank you. My wife will appreciate it."

An Unexpected Friendship

Below are examples of people waiting for ship and of a 'coffin' ship below deck where poor passengers from Ireland had only 31 inches per person and very little food. The bottom picture is another example of the crowding on these coffin ships.

DEPARTURE OF THE "NIMROD" AND "ATHLONE" STEAMERS, WITH EMIGRANTS ON BOARD, FOR LIVERPOOL.

EMIGRATION VESSEL.—BETWEEN DECKS.

THE DEPARTURE.

These sketches are in the public domain and are on the University of Waterloo's web site.

Chapter 15

Disturbing News for Josh

After helping his father with harvesting corn, Josh returned to Amherstburg in late October. One day, coming into school early, he overheard an angry Mr. Innes talking to Mr. Peden.

"And, Peden, I'll have none of your liberal ideas round my children, you hear! We believed you to be a solid church leader and now you have all these poisonous ideas. If it had'na been for James Dougall's support of you, I'd be taking my boys elsewhere. You just stick to teaching them. None of your way out theories! Do you get my meaning, man?"

"I do indeed sir. What I believe in my heart I keep for the kirk on Sundays. There is no need to come in here when I am preparing to teach. See me at the kirk in future! Good day to you, sir." As Mr. Innes left, Josh backed aside behind a wall, waited a minute, then walked in to find Mr. Peden with his head in his hands.

"Morning sir. I brought back the books you loaned Seamus."

"Put them there, Josiah. Perhaps you'd take the broom and sweep round for me."

"Yes sir," Josh replied, taking up the job quietly.

Soon the Dougall children came in followed by Henry Fry and Billy Warton, the Gordon boys and finally Duncan Innes who announced that David would not be at school that day.

The whole day went quietly as Mr. Peden went through the usual spelling, mathematics and reading with some history of Upper Canada. This interested Josh especially when Duncan asked about the new ideas for reforming the school system.

"What did Mr. Ryerson say, sir?"

"He recommended education for all and the establishment of good state schools."

"But what about separate schools?" Duncan asking as if he had prior knowledge.

"That will be up to the voters, Duncan. If the Catholics want their own school, they can establish it but I doubt they will."

"What about the coloureds?" asked Billy deliberately. Josh looked away but Henry straightened up to listen. This was an answer he needed to hear.

"We will have to see how the schools are established. Until then we'll carry on as normal. That will be all for today. I will see you tomorrow." With that the children got up from their benches and quietly left.

Outside, Josh was taunted by Billy, "See, Stokes, you'll soon have to go to your own school. We know they're talking 'bout separate schools for coloureds. My dad said so."

"And a good thing too," put in Duncan.

Just then Henry Fry came up and said, "I heard that and maybe we'll be glad to have our own school. At least we won't be bothered by the likes of you!"

Immediately Billy was on top of Henry whose slate went spinning onto the ground. Duncan looked on, laughing but Josh shouted, "Get off, Billy. Henry, don't punch back." But nothing he could do would stop the two angry boys. Soon, Mr. Peden came out of the school house and pulled them apart.

"What's all this about?" he asked.

Neither of them spoke as they wiped muck off their clothes. "You boys ought to be ashamed of yourselves! This is no way to settle arguments. Don't let me see it again! Now get on with you." Henry picked up his slate and Billy went ahead of Mr. Peden followed by Duncan Innes.

Josh said, "Henry, you'd better clean off your face afore your mama sees you, I reckon. She'd be mighty angry to see you'd been fighting."

"Well, Pa wouldn't. He says he's sick of all this wrangling round us. We better off on our own!"

"I know there's talk about separate schools, Henry, but I don't think it will be to help us. We'll have trouble finding a teacher good as Mr. Peden."

"Well my pa says Mr. Peden's a good man to us but he's got his own trouble in his church."

"How'd you know so much, Henry?" Josh asked, grimacing at him.

"I told you Josh! Pa heard he has some way out ideas but those Church people don't believe that way. It'll be his downfall, Pa says. Mr. Dougall can't be protecting him even if he's an important man."

"That's a crying shame!" exclaimed Josh banging his fist into his hand. "There's no kinder teacher anywhere. He's even helped Seamus! He's loaned him books."

"That's it man. He helps all people and some folks won't have it. Time to get off home! Bye."

"Bye Henry," Josh replied walking off with a heavy heart, determined to ask his uncle if he knew more. Back in the store, Josh got busy with chores; he filled a barrel with squash and put a sack of potatoes in front of the counter. He sniffed the fresh peppers and drying herbs above his head. His aunt had been busy that day. He also saw a new cheese out under the bell-shaped cover.

After eating some hot stew, Josh asked, "Uncle, have you heard talk about separate schools?"

"What brings that up?"

"We heard about Mr. Ryerson at school today. He's the big man in Toronto."

"Yes, I heard about him and there be talk in Parliament about reforms. It may be better to have our own school system now Josh.[4] There's more of us here and we feel we can make our own decisions that way."

"But I don't see the benefit to our children, James," added Josh's aunt. "We'll have more to pay out on books and a school building."

---

[4] In 1850 the Separate School Act came into being.

"We can use our church, first, woman. If we are free to choose, we can get us good teachers. Josh you might do that when you're older," James Alexander suggested.

"That's what Dada wants but I have more to learn. I hope we have Mr. Peden for my last two years."

"That's a mighty long time to stay at school, Josh. Come next year, your dada's going to need you on the farm. You be fourteen by then with enough schooling! I also heard tell that Mr. Robert Peden been falling into the bad books of the church. He be too liberal minded for them."

"Henry told me something like that, uncle. But Mr. Peden's a good man."

"Too good for the likes of some of them. He believes we all got chance to be saved, Josh and he preaches it real strong so I've heard. But you be telling nobody we know," said his aunt.

"I'll keep quiet, Aunt Corrie. I don't want trouble. Henry got into a fight today with Billy."

"There, James. What have I told you? Some be determined to put us down! Good for Henry I say."

"Now don't you go talking so quick, Corrie. I have to run a business here. We'll just wait and see what comes along." With those words the talk ended and Josh now understood how serious the situation was.

Chapter 16

Bad news for the Maloney Family

It was not until early December that Mr. Elliott came with some news about the immigrants from Ireland. Walking into the stable where Patrick Maloney was brushing down a horse, he said, "Hello there, Mr. Maloney, I have some news from Montreal at last but it isn't good."

"That's a pity indeed. Still tell me the worse," Patrick replied quietly.

"Most of the news coming out of Montreal is of a general nature, in the newspaper, actually," Mr. Elliott said, hesitating before going on. "It's bad. Many immigrants have come down sick on board and some have typhus. They are all being quarantined on the island called Grosse Isle and it's hard to get names. I have tried advertising for the Harte family and got nowhere."

There was silence as Patrick took this in. All he could mutter was, "I don't know how I'm going to tell my Mary. She was so looking forward to her family coming."

"I'm sorry, Patrick, if I may call you by name."

"Of course. I am much obliged to you for coming yourself. My wife is not well, you know. I may need to get help for her."

"I can recommend Dr. Grosett on Apsley Street. Tell him I gave you his name. He is a good man. Then there's Mary Scott the midwife when you need her."

"Thank you sir," Patrick Maloney said.

"Please accept my apologies for not helping you more but don't give up. I will try another advertisement," finished Mr. Elliott with an attempt at a smile.

"Thank you. We'll just pray the good Lord will keep them safe." Patrick replied quietly. "Good day to you, sir."

As Barclay Elliott left, Patrick Maloney put a harness onto the horse ready for its' owner and led the horse out. It was getting colder and he could see the horse's breath in the sharp air.

Back at the Maloney's cabin, Seamus brought in more logs for the fire. He had chopped many again that day from the trees he and his father had cleared in November. His mother sat at her loom weaving a new blanket. She was always happiest, weaving and her blankets were so soft.

"It's a fine pattern you have there, Mam," Seamus said as he passed her.

"Yes it's nice and all, although I say it myself. I've nearly finished it for the new one to come." She went back to her work while Seamus took sleepy Mary up to the room the children now shared in the loft. Mary was looking stronger and rarely coughed. She was too tired to remove anything but her outdoor shoes and stockings. Soon she was under the warm quilt shared with Dermot. Seamus went down the open steps to his mother. He had some ideas to share with her.

"Mam," he began tentatively, "I have been saving a little of my pay from Searle's. I want you to have it to buy some things you want to give the children this Christmas."

"Oh Seamus!" she said, smiling at him as she turned round. "Now isn't that kind of you, my son. I have a bit put by from selling my cheeses and that one piece of weaving to Mrs. Maloney."

"But I want you to have it Mam. I don't know what to buy Dermot and Mary. I thought maybe you'd get cloth for a dress for Mary. Mr. Dougall gets special cloth in his store near the school where Josh goes. He puts a fair price on it too. Does Dermot need boots? He's grown a lot."

"You all have, Seamus. Your da said just yesterday that you need new boots. He heard that Daniel Botsford does a fine job shoeing. Isn't that so?"

An Unexpected Friendship

"He does indeed Mam, and I have saved for my own boots too. I think I shall go to him soon before the snow comes. We could have some gifts ready for our cousins, Aunt Catherine and Uncle Joe."

"Now wouldn't that be a grand thing to do, indeed! They could come anytime. I wish we had news," his mother said hopefully pulling at her apron. They had all hoped the family would have come. Just then, as his father came in the door, Seamus looked up to see his solemn face.

"Now, Mary, how is your weaving going today?" he asked.

"I am nearly done with the job, Patrick. Have you news?"

Seamus' father sighed, sat on one chair by the fire and then spoke.

"Mr. Elliott has had no news of them but the news from Montreal is not good, Mary. I'm afraid many have gone down sick with fever." Mary Maloney took one long look at her husband and dissolved into tears. "Tell me the worse, Patrick," she urged. "Are they sick too?"

"We don't know yet. There is typhus amongst some of the immigrants. Mr. Elliott said they are kept on an island till they're well. I'm sure they are well cared for."

"Da, can't we find out more?"

"Mr. Elliott will put a special advertisement in a Montreal paper for news of them. We may hear something soon. But we must remember, the winter comes upon us soon and we may know nothing till Spring."

"Oh no Patrick! That can't be. I need my sister now."

"I know, my dear. God willing they be safe and just waiting for passage from Montreal. I heard tell of Mrs. Mary Scott today who knows what to do when it's your time, Mary. Don't fret my dear," he added kindly, putting his arm around her. "Now Seamus give us a tune to cheer us up before you go off to Searle's."

"Yes Da," Seamus replied taking out his whistle and, tapping his foot, he began a happy jig. His father soon joined in clapping but his mother just stared into the fire. Soon she had out a rosary and Seamus watched her mumbling, "Hail Mary full of grace . . ." before he left the house.

Chapter 17

December Meeting

By mid December, the roads were frozen solid and covered by a layer of snow. It was easier to travel now and Josh watched the coach hurry by on its way to Sandwich just north of their town. Tomorrow he would travel to Colchester with his uncle to bring his parents and sisters in for the special concert. Just as he was filling a candy jar, Seamus came in. "Hello there Josh. I've a list of things for my Mam. I'll read them to you," he added confidently.

"Good. Glad you came now as we be closing early tomorrow to bring my family to the concert. Have you practised that song of mine?"

"Yes, I did. I'll just follow you when you sing Josh. Together, we'll be fine. Now, I need 2 pounds flour, raisins for pudding, any cheese 8 ounces, and sugar in this tin," Seamus read, holding up a shiny can. He chatted eagerly, "I need more but I have good news to tell you. My Harte cousins be alive and Mr. Elliott heard from a reply to his advertisement!"

"That's great, Seamus. What about their mother and dad?"

"Don't know. Some doctor who treated them, told a priest who told a friend of Mr. Elliott's. Catherine, Winifred and Lizzie are in a home in Montreal now. They must be better. Mr. Elliott said the Reverend Mack knows someone there and will write to him. Mam has hope but wants to know about her sister too."

"Perhaps they will come soon. I'm glad for you Seamus. What else do you want?"

"I would like some small presents please. We sold some pork from the pigs we share with Maloneys so we've money to spare. I need two yards of bright cloth for my mother to make herself something. I like that blue stuff you have there. What's the cost?"

"It's real nice cloth and just 8 pence a yard. About one shilling and sixpence."

"Yes I have the money here," replied Seamus pulling out all his change. "They were real nice to me at Searle's last night and I been saving some."

"Good for you Seamus," Josh said as he measured out the cloth.

"Will you be getting something for your brother and little Mary?"

"Some two ounces of that candy, Josh. If I have enough, I'll take Dermot a drawing pencil and paper. He seems to love doing that."

"Right. I'll get the pencils for you to choose while I weigh out the candy." Josh watched as Seamus chose his gifts. 'How he has changed over the year,' Josh thought, smiling.

Just as they were both feeling so good, a snowball came through the small windowpane and landed on the counter.

"Who threw that?" Seamus asked and hurried to the door. Outside he watched two boys scuttling away by the church. He looked at the window pane. "Your window's broken all right! Let's put something up before the cold air comes in."

"Thanks, Seamus. I'll get my uncle." Josh walked to the back room and returned with James Alexander holding some wood in his hands.

"I see what happened Josh. Why do these boys have to go round breaking property? I shall tell Mr. Elliott about this tonight. There is no time to waste. But I'll be glad if you boys will hold this wood while I nail it across the window outside. Come put your jacket on Josh and I'll get the tools."

In the cold air, they soon had the board nailed up. Then Mr. Peden came into the store holding Billy and another boy by their collars.

"I saw what happened when I was just going into the kirk. These two tried hiding but I caught them this time. We'll have no more of this harassment if I have anything to do with it," he stated firmly glaring at both boys. "What have you to say for yourselves?"

An Unexpected Friendship

"It was Jimmy's idea this time," said Billy shuffling from foot to foot. "I was just waiting to get Seamus or Josh if they came out."

"But one of you broke my window!" exclaimed Mr. Alexander as he shook his fist at them. "This time you will pay or I'll be speaking to the magistrate tonight."

"It wasn't me, Mr. Alexander," cried Jimmy, cowering beside Mr. Peden. "Billy's lying. He put a stone in the snowball for it to go harder!" Billy's face reddened as he got furious and tried to turn on the boy.

"No you don't, young Warton. I've had enough of you," Mr. Peden commanded. "I am aware of the times you have bullied Josh and his friend. You can think what you like but I won't have violence. Mr. Alexander is a respected businessman and you repay him by breaking his window. Apologise right now and swear you'll never hurt any pupil of mine again."

Billy looked down clenching his fists as he mumbled, "Sorry. I'll pay up."

"I'll be telling your father the cost. You be working it off. Do you hear?" commanded Mr. Alexander.

"Yes. And Jimmy can help," Billy said angrily.

"That's up to you but remember you are often the ring leader, Warton," said Mr. Peden. "Now get out!"

As the two boys skulked out, Mr. Peden turned to Josh and Seamus in a more cheerful mode, saying, "Now, boys, are you two ready for the concert tomorrow?"

"Yes sir, we are. Seamus has some jigs to play and I will sing a song and recite Mr. Longfellow's poem you taught us at school."

"Which one will that be, Josh?" asked his uncle.

'I Shot an Arrow'. I know it all."

"Then let's hear it," his uncle said proudly. "You must get it right for your pa."

Josh winked at Seamus and began

"I shot an arrow into the air,
It fell to earth, I knew not where;
For, so swiftly it flew, the sight
Could not follow in its flight
I breathed a song into the air

It fell to earth, I knew not where;
For who has sight so keen and strong,
That it can follow the flight of song?

Long, long afterward, in an oak
I found the arrow, still unbroke;
And the song, from beginning to end,
I found again in the heart of a friend."

The room was quiet apart from the logs cracking in the pot-bellied stove. No one seemed to want to break the peace they felt. Then Josh added, "Mr. Longfellow wrote that on October 16 1845, uncle. It was in the Western Courier. Mr. Peden told us. Isn't it the best?"

"It's mighty fine, mighty fine, Josh," his uncle replied. "Say it first tomorrow and then sing your song."

"You're right, Mr. Alexander. The poem will set us ready for the music. Thank you for learning that so well, Josh," Mr. Peden said as he turned to leave. "I have more to prepare. Good evening to you all."

Chapter 18

The Concert

A large crowd gathered, talking happily to each other as they found seats in the old Scottish kirk next to Alexander's Store for the concert on December 17, 1846. When Mr. Peden rose, everyone quietened down.

"We are honoured tonight that so many of you have come out to enjoy this evening of recitation, music and song. We welcome our town's newly formed Fire Brigade Band." He paused as there was clapping all round and then, putting up his hand, he continued,

"Tonight, I am proud to show off some of the talents of my school children. Duncan Innes will recite for you an old poem by Robbie Burns and the Dougall family will perform a short skit with the Gordon boys from Mr. Dickens' book *A Christmas Carol*. Again there was more applause before he went on, "Before our band plays, Josiah Stokes and his new friend Seamus Maloney will join in a musical treat. Now to the concert, ladies and gentlemen."

Duncan Innes came up first, stood quietly and then said, "This is an address to Edinburgh written in 1786 by Robert Burns." After pausing, he went on

> *Edina! Scotia's darling seat!*
> *All hail thy palaces and tow'rs,*
> *Where once, beneath a Monarch's feet,*
> *Sat Legislation's sov'reign pow'rs:*

> *From marking wildly scatt 'red flowers,*
> *As on the banks of Ayr I stray'd,*
> *And singing, lone, the lingering hours,*
> *I shelter in thy honour'd shade.*

Josh looked at his father and saw him smile. 'What a moment this must be for him', he thought. 'He's now free ten years, sitting by merchants of the town, listening to poetry of a far country. I must do well for him tonight.' By the time Josh had stopped thinking happy thoughts and dreaming of a future hope, he heard Duncan finishing his sixth verse.

> *Ev'n I who sing in rustic lore,*
> *Haply my sires have left their shed,*
> *And faced grim Danger's loudest roar,*
> *Bold-following where your fathers led!*

Everyone clapped enthusiastically. Mr. Peden shook his hand before Duncan went down to sit near Josh who whispered, "That was great, Duncan!" And Duncan even smiled at Josh.

The group doing part of Mr. Dickens' Christmas Carol chose the story when young Scrooge was alone after other boys leave the schoolroom at Christmas and his sister came to take him home. It was moving and the audience showed their appreciation by remaining silent until the group bowed.

Mr. Peden nodded at Josh next to recite his poem. He saw his mother and aunt wiping their eyes as he finished. Then Josh said, "My friend Seamus Maloney and I have a song for you." Seamus played part of the tune as an introduction before Josh came in with

> *There is a balm in Gilead*
> *To make the wounded whole;*
> *There is a balm in Gilead*
> *To heal the sin sick soul. (The refrain)*

> *Sometimes I feel discouraged,*
> *And think my work's in vain,*
> *But then the Holy Spirit*
> *Revives my soul again. (The refrain)*

An Unexpected Friendship

Don't ever feel discouraged,
for Jesus is your friend,
and if you look for knowledge
He'll ne'er refuse to lend. (The refrain)

Soon folk were overcome with tears hearing this beautiful old melody and they applauded long. Josh and Seamus stepped down as Mr. Peden rose to announce the last group. "The Fire Brigade Band will play some well known tunes and you are welcome to join in. We all wish you a blessed Christmas time."

The Band first played the popular Scottish song, Charlie is ma Darling; then a march before Christians Awake! Salute the Happy Morn which some people knew. After two verses, they finished with O Come All Ye Faithful; it was sung vigorously by most of the audience. Although new to Josh, he soon picked up the chorus and sang along. Seamus nudged him, saying, "I must learn those tunes now as I'll be asked to play them at Searle's, I reckon."

It was a wonderful way to end the night. As they left, Mr. Innes came to Josh and said in his broad Scots voice, "You've a grand voice there, laddie. I always enjoy a gud song! Aye. Try some of Robbie Burns' fine songs next time."

"Thank you sir," replied Josh. "I would be glad to learn them."

"I'll have my Davie tell you the words then. Gud night to you." With those kind words, Mr. Innes took his wife's arm and went out, followed by his two sons.

Josh was surprised and so pleased that he put his arm round Seamus' shoulder. Next both boys looked for their families and Seamus brought his over to meet Mr. and Mrs. Stokes, Josh's aunt Alexander and his sisters. After polite introductions, Mrs. Alexander said, "Oh what a splendid evening! Do come to our house for a hot drink, Mrs. Maloney, before you go back on the wagon. My sister and her family are staying with us."

"Thank you," replied Seamus' mother. "A hot drink would be welcome on this cold night." Seamus couldn't have been happier. Picking up Dermot, he kissed him. Angeline and Corrie Stokes skipped out beside their aunt, asking her, "Can we have some cookies now, Auntie Corrie?"

"'Spect so, if I can find them," she teased. Mary hung back by her mother till Josh said, "Come with me. I'll show you the way."

This section of Amherstburg's Map of 1845 shows the dock area where the school was. Back on Bathhurst Street is the Church (at #4) where the concert was and next door (at # 5) Mr Alexander's store. The tinsmith's workshop was also near the Dougal Wharf.

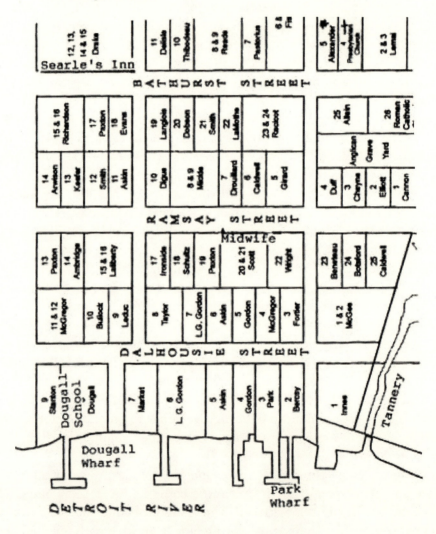

Chapter 19

Fire at the Dock

In January, David Innes brought the words of two songs to school. He gave them to Mr. Peden to give Josh, using the excuse that his teacher would need to teach Josh the tunes. He added, "My father wants Stokes to sing them at your Robbie Burns' concert at the end of the month."

"He'll learn them; his friend Seamus will get the music," replied Mr. Peden.

As a result, Seamus and Josh found themselves back in the old kirk on a very cold night at the end of January 1847. But it was the same night that Seamus' mother was so sick. She was near her time so his father called in the midwife Mary Scott. Seamus didn't want to leave his dear mother but his father insisted.

"Your Mam will be in good hands Seamus. I've seen her like this before and I think the babe may come early. Now don't you be worrying! Go and play your best."

"Then I'll go, Da but come back quickly."

When he got to the store, Josh said, "Seamus I've been practising today and sometimes my voice gives out like it's cracking!"

His uncle said, "I heard you Josh. That happens. You be thirteen come Spring."

Josh smiled and stood up straighter, "That must be it uncle."

"I hear your voice changing too, Seamus. It's natural like. Now you'll be grown friends. I'm right pleased Josh met you."

"Thank you, sir. Josh sure helped me to learn. I can now read all the signs, *The Courier** and enjoy the books he brings."

"Good for you. Now off you two go and I'll be thinking of you." These kindly words stayed with the boys as they entered the church. Inside they saw David and Duncan Innes, Robert Gordon and Tom Duff. Mr. Innes approached them, a broad smile on his ruddy face. "Och, here you are. Ready to sing I hope."

"I'll try, sir but my voice seems to be changing," Josh replied.

"You'll do it. Just expect to do it well," Mr. Innes said, "Now sit yourselves dun."

So Josh and Seamus found themselves sitting next to David Innes who whispered, "I'm reciting a poem tonight." Josh smiled back and wished him well.

Just then Mr. Elliott got up and said, "Welcome to the Literary Society's Special Night to honour our Scottish heritage. I am delighted to be invited to welcome our young performers and our Fire Brigade Band again." Everyone clapped and the band began to play.

After two cheerful tunes, they stopped and David Innes got up to say his poem. His father watched him, mouthing many of the words along with his son, Josh noted. Josh liked Mr. Innes more each time he met him.

It was now Seamus' turn to play a tune; he played Auld Lang Syne because he'd played it at Searle's. Everyone clapped. Then Josh went up to the front to join him. He stood quietly as Seamus played the chorus. The audience smiled, recognizing the tune and Josh began to sing,

> *"Twas on a Monday morning,*
> *Right early in the year,*
> *That Charlie came to our town,*
> *The young Chevalier.*
> *-An' Charlie, he's my darling,*
> *My darling, my darling,*
> *Charlie, he's my darl . . ."*

But he could not finish. One man burst into the room, shouting,

An Unexpected Friendship

"Dougall's wharf's on fire! Come quickly!"

Now panic set in. James and John Dougall rushed out followed by Mr. Innes, Mr. Peden and all the Fire Brigade. Robert Gordon shouted to the boys, "Follow me. There's the side window. We can climb out." Robert pushed open the window and helped each boy jump out through it.

"My uncle will lend buckets," shouted Josh. "Let's get some!" But the store was already full of men taking buckets. The boys followed the crowd to the fire.

It was a strong one as the wind had fanned the flames. The whole dock, made of timbers, was at risk. Men were breaking ice at the end of the wharf to get the water from the river. Buckets were quickly filled and soon passed along the chain of men towards the burning school house. The fire brigade with the only fire-dowser in town, had not yet arrived.

When they came, they had to push people aside to get to the water.

"Clear the way now!" demanded Mr. Allanson Botsford who was usually a quiet Quarter Sessions clerk. The volunteer brigade took the solitary water pipe and pump up to the river. Mr. McLeod threw one end into the water and two men started to pump while others took the hose closer to the buildings.

"Aim it at the store," someone shouted. "Keep it wet so we can get some goods out."

Josh watched his uncle tie a wet cravat around his face before he rushed into the building. Another black man followed him and the two were soon dragging out a large box. Others followed suit and brought out bolts of cloth and more boxes.

They all worked furiously for an hour but could not stop the flames spreading. Suddenly they heard a crack in the roof; it was about to collapse. When the boys moved back, they saw Billy Warton smiling at the edge of the crowd. He seemed to be enjoying the blaze!

The exhausted men could do no more. As the burning timbers came down, one man threw himself into the icy river, swam to the next wharf and got hauled out. People were thrown backwards by the heat into Dalhousie Street; others ran away.

Just then, Mr. Michael Maloney came up to Seamus, "You're to come home with me now, me boy. No more hanging round here." Seamus followed without a word, remembering his mother again.

The Fire Brigade kept up the water pressure using volunteers into the early hours of the next day. In the grey light of January, losses were quite evident. James Dougall's store was a ruin. Everything in the school house was burned to the ground; only the small stove and the metal globe stand showed, blackened by the fierce heat.

The tinsmith's workshop held nothing but charred bits of metal, blackened tools and a mangled wood stove.

Later that morning, Josh asked his uncle, "Can I go and find out about the school?"

"I'll come too. There'll be work to do, cleaning up. I'll tell your aunt we're going."

They strode silently down the Gore to Dalhousie Street; then they turned towards Market Square. There Mr. Dougall was speaking t Mr. Peden and a few parents.

"I'm afraid that's the end of this school," he sighed. "I'll have to concentrate my efforts on the Sandwich Store now. We can't afford to rebuild here. There's always a risk of fire among these wooden structures."

"You're right there, James," said Mr. Gordon. "But we've never had trouble till now. I wonder if someone had it in for your school. There's been plenty of talk."

"I know that but I do my best for this town. I don't think I have enemies!" James Dougall protested.

"But I do," said his cousin, Robert Peden quietly. "There's many a man who has had words with me about my liberal views. I feel I'm to blame, cousin."

"Now, Robert, don't you be vexing yourself. It could have been an accident. See how mangled that stove looks in the tinsmith's place. Maybe the logs sparked or fell out there. We'll never know."

Josh listened to all this with interest and thought of Billy Warton's face the night before. He looked as if he had been enjoying the fire. Would he go that far to get Josh and Henry out of the school? It was hard to believe even though Josh knew how he felt about coloured people in town.

Mr. Dougall turning to Josh's uncle, said, "I have to thank you for going into the store last night. You and your friends saved a bundle of cloth and other goods."

"Oh that was nothing," Mr. Alexander said shyly." I've done it before. I remembered how we did it back in Kentucky when the old store house was a-burning."

"I'm much obliged to you anyway and, if I can pass on some goods you could use, I'd be glad to," said Mr. Dougall.

"No need for that, sir. Glad to help."

Just then, Mr. Fry came up with Henry and asked if they could help clear up. Soon many men and boys were loading charred lumber into Tom Fry's cart. After an hour or so, Josh and his uncle started back to the store and met Seamus.

"Hello there, Josh. I've news," he called. They stopped and Josh asked, "What is it Seamus?"

"I won't forget the night of the fire ever," Seamus replied, smiling broadly. Then he explained, "It was the same night my new baby sister was born. She's to be Kathleen like my grandma."

"That's good news, Seamus. How's your mother?" Mr. Alexander asked.

"She come through it but she looks real pale. Mrs. Scott said she's to stay in bed. Mrs. Maloney's with her now. I came by for the tea, she's asking for."

"Then we'll get it for you right away," said Josh's uncle. "Come with us."

Here is a picture of Christ Church Amherstburg where the Reverend Frederick Mack was rector during this time. The Church was built in 1816.

Chapter 20

Learning

Throughout the winter months, Josh and Seamus met and read whatever they could find. Seamus kept reading the Western Courier which was pinned up to a board by the inn where he still worked. He kept hoping to find good news about his Irish relatives. Josh had enjoyed teaching Seamus so much that he now helped young Mary read. He found her a keen student. Once Spring came, she seemed much stronger and was coughing less. Mary enjoyed reading poetry and loved it when Josh sang to her. She even laughed when his voice suddenly changed. "You sounded like an old bear then," Mary teased one day.

Josh laughed but added, "Then I'll have to give you a big bear hug!"

Instantly Mary ran away to her mother who smiled and asked,

"What's happening here now?" Josh saw that Mrs. Maloney was more out going since the new baby was born.

"Oh Josh was teasing me because I told him his voice was funny," Mary answered.

"That's no way to thank your teacher. Now, be telling him about the school, Mary."

Josh looked up as Mary said, "I'm to go to the new small school, Mrs. Reilly has for us. Isn't that grand Josh! What will you be doing now?"

"I'll go back to my parents. They have a farm and my pa could use my help soon."

"We'll miss you, Josh," said Mrs. Maloney. "But you'd make a good teacher."

"I'd like to do that, ma'am but I'm near fourteen now and must think of working."

After saying goodbye to the family, Josh walked the long road into town. He felt much more confident now. He had made friends with David Innes and Billy was kept so busy by his father that he didn't have time to bother anyone. Josh had grown a good three inches and his work in the store had given him bigger muscles.

He knew he could move on now with the knowledge that he could survive bullying.

Just as he was thinking all this, Josh met Mr. Peden. "Afternoon, Josiah. Glad I met you. The Literary Society is hoping to set up a public library sometime soon."

"That is good news, sir. I hope we can use it too."

"We shall see, Josiah. It is needed especially as I have no time to teach anymore. The building of the new St. Andrew's Kirk takes so much time. It'll be a fine building but I do not hold out hopes of staying there."

"Why not, sir?" asked Josh

"I have strong beliefs, Josiah," he replied. "I read God's word and I'm convinced He wants to save us all not just the elect! You'll hear people are against me but I've not changed my mind a bit. I see that there is much to do to educate people. Mark my words, they'll have me out soon.[5]"

"Mr. Peden, I hope not. You've taught us so much. Your nephews still need you."

"Thank you Josiah. But cousin James is sending them to schools in Sandwich this Spring so I'll not be needed. Now, you are worth teaching and I know that there's a good school up in Buxton where you could become a pupil teacher and learn more there. Do you think you are about ready to take that step?"

---

[5] Robert Peden was tried for heresy by his church in 1850. He had already formed the Evangelical Union and moved to Hamilton, Ontario

Josh looked right into Mr Peden's eyes and said, "I'd liked to try that, sir. I must ask my pa to find out if he needs me."

"I understand that. You could go after planting is done, Josh. I'm sure your father and your uncle would approve. It will be a chance to see more of this world."

"I'd like that. And Buxton[6] is only a half day's journey from the New Settlement. Can you recommend me?" "I certainly will. I have to see Reverend King who established the school. I'll let you know in a month or so. I must go now."

"Thank you sir and thank you for lending me books," Josh answered.

Early in April the weather broke and Josh and Seamus saw that more boats were moving on the River Detroit. The Park Brothers had taken over the Dougall wharf and had several cords of wood on it ready for their new steamer, Earl Cathcart. This year the number of steamers, schooners and smaller boats coming into Amherstburg had grown. There was a good daily service to Detroit, one to Buffalo and another across the lake to Ohio. The Parks export business was flourishing and Mr. Innes talked about building a stronger wharf.

"You know Josh, I'd love to work on a boat and see something more of the world," Seamus exclaimed. He'd filled out a bit in the past year and had got stronger from all the farming work he'd done with the Maloneys.

"Why do you fancy that, Seamus?" Josh asked

"I think it's got something to do with my granda in Ireland. He was a sailor; he was pressed into it first, he said, but then he got to like the life and that's where he learned to play the tin whistle."

"That's how come he had so much time to practice!" Josh teased.

"That's not how it was at all! Times there was no sleep but it sounded grand to me. My da is goin' to ask if I can be a deck hand for Mr. Parks when he sees him."

---

[6] Buxton had a fine school for many years attended by black students first but others joined later.

Chapter 21

A New Experience

About a month later, as the two boys came out of Alexander's store, they saw Rev. Mack hurrying towards them waving his hands madly about in the air. Josh had just given Seamus a new volume of Poems by Mr. Longfellow to read to Mary and was telling him about the poet when Reverend Mack came closer. He had charge of Christ Church on Ramsey Street. Josh was wondering if he wanted them to deliver a message when he spoke.

"I have news for your family, Seamus," the small rotund clergyman said, breathing heavily. "Mr. Elliott's contact in Montreal has told us that your Harte cousins were removed this winter to the Toronto Asylum. It's a charitable place for those in need and they would have been well cared for."

"Thank you sir. That's wondrous news. But what of my aunt or uncle?"

"I fear we must assume that all is not well. The typhoid's a terrible disease and it took many. But I'm only guessing. I came to tell you that I am willing to offer help for the three girls. I can give the oldest work in my home and I'm sure your family will be glad to have your other two until they find posts. Please let your father know of my interest. I could not go as far as the inn today. Tell him to come and see me and we'll arrange details soon."

"Sure you're real kind, sir. My mother will be over the moon to have Catherine and Elizabeth with her and to see Winnie again. She's still not strong and they'll be good help with a new baby in The house. I'll run to tell my Da now."

"You do that. No need to hurry. I'm glad I saw you," Reverend Mack said. "I have to write back to the Asylum. They want a confirmation from your father for me to take with me."

"I will and all!" Seamus said, hurrying off. "See you soon Josh. Thanks for the book."

In the two months that followed, Seamus heard nothing but there was plenty to do in May with planting and Josh had gone back to his parents' farm to work.

One day in early July, Seamus rushed into the store and said,

"Mr. Alexander, will Josh be back sometime? I'm to go with Reverend Mack to bring my cousins here in two week's time. I just wanted to let Josh know."

"He could be visiting us by then. If planting's done, his mama likes to visit her sister, Mrs. Alexander to see about canning. If Tom Fry is going that way, I'll give him a message for you."

"Thanks, Mr. Alexander, I'd sure like to see Josh afore we go. Reverend Mack says the girls would feel happier if I was with him.

Mr. Parks has offered him free passage to Toronto on his steamer the Earl Cathcart and said I can work."

"That's wonderful Seamus. I saw that boat being built. Josh told me you fancy working on board. Perhaps you can entertain them and see how they like it."

"That's a good idea Mr. Alexander. I'll see you if Josh comes in a few days."

"Fine. And if you need food for the journey, you know where to come!"

Somehow, Josh got word of Seamus' news and within a week, he'd come with his mother and sisters to Amherstburg. "Can I go and see if Seamus is working at the inn, Mama?" Josh asked as soon as they arrived.

"Of course, son. But you be back here soon so we can eat together."

"Right, Mama." Off Josh went as quickly as he could. He found Mr. Maloney in the livery stables and heard that Seamus was to be down to play soon.

"You just stay here, Josh. Seamus always comes in before he goes to play inside. Hot night now isn't it? I'll never get used to these mosquitoes!" Mr. Maloney added, slapping one off his cheek.

"After working outdoors with my pa near the sulphur springs, they don't seem so bad here." Josh replied. Then he heard footsteps and saw Seamus beaming at him.

"Josh, my friend, what do you think about my trip by boat? Wish you could come."

"Really? I could ask. I've done all I can to help my pa and I haven't got to start at the Buxton school till Fall now. Would I be allowed to come? It costs you know."

"Reverend Mack travels free like all the ministers and I am going to work my passage. Perhaps they'd use another deck hand. I can always ask."

"That'd be great, Seamus. I could see the Welland canal and find out how long it takes to get to Toronto from here. It would be an educational experience. My ma might let me go." Josh was now quite excited and added, "I'll go and ask my family right now and you can check with us after you play."

With that, Josh disappeared down the road to his uncle's store.

He immediately explained about the journey to Toronto and the possibility that he could go. But his aunt, uncle and mother looked sad and anxious.

"What's the matter?" Josh inquired. His uncle replied in a serious tone, "It's risky for you to go on board, Josh 'cause of your colour. You know that yourself."

"But, uncle, many coloured folk work on boats. The Pearl brings people to freedom and Mr. Parks is a rich merchant. His boats stay on the Canadian side."

"I see your point but I think most trips go to Buffalo, New York. It's up to your mother now to give you permission to go. What do you think, Carrie?"

"You're my only son Josh and I worry for you. Could be a danger on them boats."

"But I'm careful, Mama and strong enough to help on board. If Mr. Parks agrees, can I go? I'd learn so much in a short time," Josh urged.

"We'll see what Mr. Parks says. Your uncle will go along with you tomorrow. Let's eat now. Come in girls, Auntie Rose has supper ready. Wash up."

Early the next day, Josh headed down to the dock with his uncle. Mr. Parks was in his office when they came in.

"Mornin' Alexander," said Mr. Parks,

"Mornin' to you, sir. Josh has a question for you."

"Well, out with it boy. Haven't got much time today. I've got to do some hiring for our next trip out."

"Would that be for the Earl Cathcart, sir?" Josh asked.

"Yes, it is. Why? Are you interested in being a deck hand? Are you strong enough to help load her?" Mr Parks inquired. "I'd like to try, sir. My friend Seamus Maloney says he will be working the voyage as far as Toronto and would be glad of my company. I've worked on my pa's farm and I'm not afraid of hard work."

"That's true, Mr. Parks," added Josh's uncle. "You may know he worked for me while he was schooled by Mr. Peden."

"Yes I did know of that. Well, I'll watch you load her Josh. We begin in one day. Work hard and I'll take you on."

"There's just one point, sir. How's the risk for Josh, being coloured and all?"

"No worry there, Alexander. Anyone working on my boats is protected by me. I'll see to that. I'm against slavery. Anyone on my boat is as safe as being in Canada."

"Thank you sir. That will put his mother's fears at rest."

"Thank you, sir," added Josh, hardly able to stand still. He was anxious to share the news with Seamus.

When they got back to the store, Josh's uncle said, "It's all right. Josh will be fine. He deserves this chance. Mr. Parks' said his ship's captain will protect Josh."

"So I can go, Mama?" Josh asked again to be sure.

"Yes, of course and my prayers will keep you safe too," his mother replied.

When Seamus came in the next night, the two friends talked excitedly. "How long will we be away?" Josh asked.

"Could be ten days or more. Much depends on the canal, the sailors say. We may have to change boats there. I'm not sure."

An Unexpected Friendship

"Whatever happens it will be exciting. I just hope I pass the loading test," Josh said. Then he added, "What about food?" "We can take some extras but basic rations go with the job," Seamus answered.

"You seem to have it all in hand, Seamus," said Mr. Alexander.

"I found out all I can, Mr. Alexander. The journey will go best for me if Josh comes along and I want to work on a boat myself."

The next morning, at first light, Josh strode down to the dock and waited to be called to take a load on board. His first loads were bales of wheat which he was used to handling. Seamus was given a similar bundle and they both worked hard with different loads for some two hours before the hot sun made them all need a break and the captain called a short stop. By then the sweat was pouring down across their eyes. Josh's uncle had sent him with bread, cheese and a drink so he and Seamus ate hungrily and they drank the good cool apple cider.

"That was just right, Josh. Don't forget the food for tomorrow, for sure," Seamus teased, smiling at Josh. At the end of the day, Captain Bury came up to them and said,

"Well done. You worked hard as any man today. Welcome aboard. We'll be sailing by 9 o'clock tomorrow to make Port Burwell by evening."

"Thank you, sir," they both said almost bowing to the well-known captain. "We'll be here in good time tomorrow."

"You'll hear the steamer's whistle when she's ready to board about eight of the clock. I'll see you then," added the captain as he dismissed them.

A Map of the Journey to Toronto in 1847

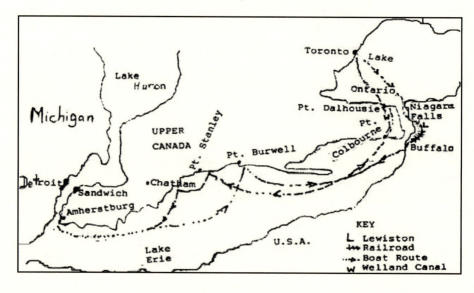

Chapter 22

All on Board

The next day they watched as Reverend Mack boarded the ship,
"Mornin' boys. I see you're ready to go!" he said, chuckling as he passed on to his cabin. Some others came aboard before Seamus and Josh helped two seamen pull up the gang plank. Soon they would be on their way! They both grinned at each other, their chests puffed out with pride at being deck hands on a steamer heading for Toronto. Their delight was noted by the kindly old Reverend who pointed them out to the Captain's mate.
Within the hour, they were steaming along Lake Erie, protected by a canvas awning from the smoking funnel and the noisy propeller. This was quite an experience, Josh thought and he shouted to Seamus, "It's real noisy on board!"
"What did you say?" Seamus bellowed, holding a hand round one ear. "I'll come back to you." As Seamus walked along the deck two busy seamen were already at work. One said, "You two report to the lower deck for your jobs today. Right now."
"Aye, aye, sir," replied Seamus as he pulled Josh's arm to come.
The young boys were kept busy below deck sweeping and polishing for some hours. On a short break they were allowed to come up and they saw how huge Lake Erie was.

"All I can see is water, Seamus. There's no sign of land now. I think Lake Erie is 210 miles long and 57 miles wide. It looks like the sea!"

"You're right there! Reminds me of the weeks on the awful 'coffin' ship, Dealey from Cork! I never thought we'd reach land!" Seamus exclaimed. "It was terrible, Josh. There must have been over three hundred of us at first but many died. The little food we had to eat had grubs in it. It made my brother and sister so sick. That and the foul air below deck."

"Don't dwell on it now, Seamus. We're lucky to have the food we need now. I hope your cousins are well when we find them."

"So do I. It'll be a while afore we get there though."

One sailor heard them and shouted over, "You'll be seeing the north shore of Erie soon enough. We made good time today so we'll be in Port Burwell to take on cargo by evening. Make the most of your break. You'll be busy then!"

"Thanks for telling us," Seamus cried back. "Would you like to hear a jig?"

"I would indeed. It'll help to pass the time," replied the sailor.

Seamus began to play one of the cheerful jigs he knew and the tune was so catchy that a couple of sailors started to dance. Soon, a few passengers came to look and clap to the music. Even the captain poked his head out to see what was going on. Since there was not much to do, he smiled and let the dancing go on. Seamus moved from one jig to another until the men tired of dancing.

"That was fun to watch," said Josh. "Now I see how popular your grandfather may have been."

"Yes, he enjoyed the long voyages when there was time to play. He went all the way to Spain, you know," said Seamus proudly. By dusk, the boys were cleaning the upper deck when they saw the large wooden lighthouse as the steamer came closer to Port Burwell. Then they brought up sacks of salted pork and a few bales of wheat. The hour at the port passed as they all had plenty to do.

Before long they were away again with more wood on board to fuel the steamer. The steamer journeyed on through the night so the boys were able to look at the stars as they chose to sleep up on deck. It was a fine night and Josh was thrilled watching for Venus and other stars in the night sky.

"You know a lot Josh. Wish I'd been able to get on deck more when on the old boat. We were that stuffed into awful bunks below deck without any hope of feeling the fresh air at night."

"You're still angry about all that, aren't you, Seamus?"

"I think I will be for a long time, Josh and, coming on board here made me think of it all again. Ah well, but I'm that tired now. Goodnight Josh."

The next morning the boys were up at first light, woken by the steamer's whistle of one long and two short hoots as it neared the entry into the Welland Canal.

"Not anything you can do now, boys," said a seaman. "Have to be patient here. There are twenty-seven locks to go through and it'll be tight in some, I dare say!"

"Thanks for telling us," Josh replied as he moved to the front of the deck to watch with Seamus.

They saw a long narrow pier with a small lighthouse at one end as the steamer entered the first lock. Within the hour the boys had watched as the water in the first lock went down some eight feet.

Then the boat was let out into the next lock which it seemed to almost fill in breadth. The lock was 220 feet and, once their steamer was in, the water was reduced again and the boys could feel the motion under them as the Earl Cathcart dropped down to the next level. There they had to wait as another smaller boat was in the next lock.

Reverend Mack came alongside them and remarked, "This could take a day or two Seamus but then, we'll be just four hours out of Toronto at Port Dalhousie. This bigger steamer has to go through as slowly as any other boat, you know."

"But it's interesting to watch the locks, isn't it sir?" asked Seamus.

"Yes it is son. Glad you see it that way." With that said, he left them to watch.

It took another hour before they got through the third lock. Seamus and Josh watched as the rest of the day was spent going through twenty more locks. Since they were stalled till first light, most on board slept. Shortly after six o'clock, the steamer made its way through the last seven locks. Seamus walked up and down the deck unable to relax, straining his eyes towards distant buildings.

It would take another four hours before they came out into Lake Ontario at Port Dalhousie.

"You must be getting excited, Seamus," Josh remarked.

"Sure I am, Josh. It'll be grand to see my cousins again. You'll like Catherine; she's your age, then there's Lizzie. But our Winnie is nicest; she used to tell me stories of Cuchulain many a time. They lived near us back home," Seamus replied.

"Boys, come, eat and then you can help with clean up," their friendly seaman said.

Down in the lower deck, they shared bread and some cheese with the sailors followed by a hot tea. Then Josh and Seamus were told to scrub off the table and sweep around. The others went to check the cargo they had to unload in Toronto.

The short journey to the port at Toronto took another four hours but the boys were able to be up on deck as they came into the harbour. They saw many different kinds of boats and had to have a small tug boat guide them into the Brown's wharf to dock. This was quite a tricky manoeuvre but the Earl Cathcart was docked by the afternoon

The boys now had some of their heaviest work, unloading cargo of salt beef, tobacco, grains and some fine lumber. This was their last task on board.

"You'll have your work cut out now," said Reverend Mack. "I'll go and find the Asylum and return for you later, Seamus."

"Thank you. Sure it will be grand to have news of my cousins."

A view of Toronto in 1846.

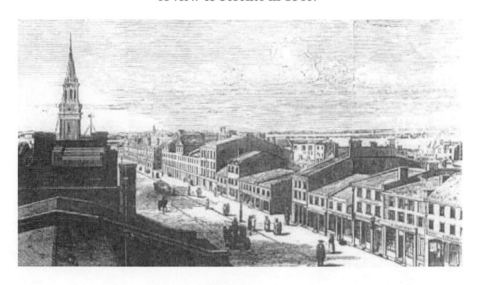

Below it is a typical steam ship of about 1840.

Both prints are in the public domain.

Chapter 23

Two Families Reunited

As the men put the gang plank down, Reverend Mack hurried off the boat. Then he marched up the hill looking at his watch before putting it back into his upper pocket. He was an imposing sight in his black clerical suit and large brimmed hat. He strode with determination to complete his mission to find the Harte girls. The two boys watched him go out of sight in between hauling loads off the steamer.

It was evening when the reverend returned, looking a little dishevelled from his efforts but smiling happily as he called,

"Seamus, I found them. You'll see them soon."

Seamus laughed and jumped for joy. "To see my cousins again! How grand!"

It was only on the next morning that they could follow the reverend across the dock and up a steep bank where all kinds of people were crowded. Josh noted how poor and lost some looked. "They'll be new immigrants, I warrant," said Seamus, pointing at a family of five in shabby tattered clothes. They looked forlorn and fearful sitting on an old trunk. Seamus smiled as he tipped his cap.

"They look just like us when we got off our long journey," Seamus whispered.

"But you're doing well Seamus and soon we'll fi nd your cousins," Josh encouraged.

Reverend Mack marched ahead and the boys had to hustle to catch him up. They turned into Queen Street and hurried along to another side street before stopping at a large wooden building. Seamus looked up at the sign and read, "Toronto Asylum for Widows and Orphans. This is it. I'll see my cousins soon. Hurrah!"

"Let's go in," said Reverend Mac. "We're expected as I arranged yesterday to collect your cousins."

It was now eight o'clock and inside, the boys watched as a stream of young children came out across the hall. Suddenly, an older girl broke away and called out, "Seamus is that really you?"

"Winnie!" Seamus exclaimed. A thin girl ran to him, tears just streaming down her face. "Oh Seamus, it's been so long since we saw any of our own kind! Now you've found us. Praise the Lord!"

"Amen to that," said Reverend Mack.

"Catherine, Lizzie, come here. Seamus has come for us!"

"Well, it's really Reverend Mack who brought us, Winnie," Seamus explained.

"Thank you kindly sir," Winnie said, curtseying a little.

"And here be my sisters."

"How do you do, girls," Reverend Mack said in a cheerful voice as he smiled warmly at the three girls.

"Who be this lad, Seamus?" Catherine asked.

"Oh, this is Josh Stokes from our town, Amherstburg. He came to keep me company."

"Good day to you all," Josh murmured. Then he watched Seamus hug his two younger cousins.

Rev. Mack coughed to get their attention before stating, "I need to see the administrator in charge before we can take the girls. You wait here, Josh while Seamus and I go into the officer's room to sort things out. He told me he has to see you too. Girls, you need to come too. Business first, talk after."

Some minutes later they all returned; the youngest girl was skipping along and she came right up to Josh to say, "You don't know but I have two names, Mary Elizabeth. Here I'm Mary and now Seamus is come, I can be Lizzie again!" And she laughed with pleasure.

"Catherine, Lizzie, Mrs. Barton said we can go and get our things. Remember?" Winnie reminded them.

"We won't be long Seamus," said Catherine who looked anxiously at her cousin.

The girls almost ran up the dark stairway, bumping into a young woman who was washing down steps. "Watch where you're goin'," she said, glowering at them. They apologised and were soon out of sight.

Seamus was on edge, hopping from foot to foot until he saw little Lizzie come down with her small bundle followed by Catherine and Winnie.

"I'll help carry your bundles," Josh offered taking them from the two younger girls.

Seamus took Winnie's arm as she clung to his side, saying, "Oh Seamus, it's so good to be with family again. We felt lost when our mam died." Now Seamus, Josh and Reverend Mack knew for certain that the girls were alone.

Seamus had to ask, "What about your Da?"

"He got sick on the boat over; he kept throwing up and he had an awful fever. We couldn't do anything for him. No one would help; they were all too scared of the fever. It was terrible trying to look after him in that awful hole. There was no fresh air. We'd hardly breathe. My Da just got worse and by the twelfth day out, he just lay on his bed, rambling. It was awful to see him, Seamus. I can't bear to think on it!" With that she broke into a flood of tears.

With tears in his eyes, Seamus said, "Now, Winnie. All that's done with and you're safe with us. My Mam and Da love you like their own. We'll be together from now on."

"That we will," said Catherine boldly, adding, "And no more bread and milk suppers I hope!"

"I'll have none of that Catherine. 'Tis kind people like Mrs. Barton that took us in, gave us shelter and told Uncle Patrick we were here."

"Well now we have you, we must be practical," said Rev. Mack.

"We have to leave this place now. Do you wish to say goodbye?"

"I'd like to see one friend I made," said Catherine. "She helps in the kitchen. Shall I go now?"

"Yes, go quickly," he replied. "And what about you, Winifred?"

"I'd like to thank Mrs. Barton again, sir. I'll just be a minute. Come along Lizzie."

The two hurried off to the small office and came out soon with Mrs. Barton's arm around little Lizzie. She said, "Winifred is a good worker Reverend. I shall be sorry to loose her."

"Well, that is a good recommendation for her indeed," said the kindly gentleman smiling as he looked at the girls, contented that he had found them so easily. "We are indebted to you, ma'am for the good work you do here. Now come along everyone. Good day to you, ma'am."

Once Catherine had joined them, they all left the building. In a business like voice, Reverend Mack said, "We need extra food for the journey home back. We can't return on the Earl Cathcart, as you know boys. I heard that the Queen Victoria sails out at 2 pm for Niagara and Lewiston. Then we'll get the connecting rail car to Buffalo. Now let's get food."

"I can smell a bakery nearby," Josh said sniffing the air. "I think it's that way, sir."

So the small party of six, set off to buy fresh bread. Seamus found a general store and bought a chunk of cheese. They were ready to go back to the dock.

Chapter 24

The Journey Home to Amherstburg

Once they reached the wharf, a man told them, "The Queen's always in by noon." Josh took out a book to read while Seamus was chatting with his young cousins. Soon, they saw the Queen Victoria making her way into shore.

When it had docked and let off passengers, it was open to those waiting to take the crossing to Niagara. When Captain Hugh Richardson saw the reverend, he waved him on board and the other five followed.

"Good day sir. We need fares for the crossing to Lewiston," stated Reverend Mack. "I have here three immigrants and two young men. All will stay on deck."

"That will be $5.00, sir. You are, of course, free. We should be there at 6 o'clock in time for the rail cars to Buffalo."

"That's just what we need," replied the clergyman as he handed over the money.

One deck hand hollered, "All aboard now, sailing for Niagara, Queenston and Lewiston within the hour."

"Oh, this boat is lovely!" Lizzie shrieked with joy as she ran along the deck.

"Be careful, Lizzie," Winnie warned but she was smiling.

"This is grand, Seamus," she whispered. "Soon we'll see Auntie Mary." When all passengers were on board, the Queen Victoria pulled away. The girls waved joyously to people on the dock even though they got no response.

"Goodbye to all that," said Lizzie, pushing her hands in front of her. "I can't wait to see little Mary and Dermot. Seamus, are they as big as me now?"

"Not yet, Lizzie but Mary's growing well. She's so pleased you are coming. We have another little sister Kathleen too. She's only six months old."

"Oh that's exciting," put in Catherine. "I love babies."

"Then my ma will be glad to have you around," laughed Seamus.

Josh noticed that Winnie walked apart from the others, wiping her eyes with her fresh clean pinafore. She had had to watch out for her two sisters for some months; Josh guessed, she needed time to be alone.

During the four hour trip across the lake, they enjoyed the sights they made out along the shore and the nice cooler evening breeze. Seamus was often conversing with his two eldest cousins so Josh entertained young Lizzie. He saw that she would be lively company for Seamus' sister, Mary. She skipped ahead of him and was soon engrossed in all the sights Josh could show her. She particularly liked watching the shapes the water made at the back of the boat.

"Is that ever wonderful," she remarked to Josh. "I never saw that happen on the ocean. We couldn't stay on deck long."

"Then enjoy it all now Lizzie. We'll go by rail car next to Buffalo. By morning, we'll be on a steamer in Lake Erie. You'll see our town in two or three days, I reckon."

They enjoyed the food later on and were thrilled when Josh brought out the candy sticks he'd been saving.

"What a treat this is," said Catherine." You guessed what I'd like!"

"And me," chirped up Lizzie. "I never tasted anything so good."

"Then I'll tell my uncle. They are a gift from him," Josh answered.

"I'm going to make mine last a long time!" exclaimed Lizzie. Captain Richardson was quite right and the boat docked at Lewiston before six that evening. Alongside the dock were the rail cars waiting for new passengers.

"I've never been on a train before!" exclaimed the girls together.

"Nor have I," echoed Josh.

"Me neither," said Seamus. "It will be fun!"

"It is an efficient way to get us to Buffalo for the next boat to Detroit. It's not a long trip—about 12 miles. We use it to bi-pass the Niagara Falls," explained the reverend.

After debarking at Milloy's dock, they crossed to the railroad tracks. There, Reverend Mack gave some money for their fares to Buffalo and they all got into one train car. Josh had some anxious moments and asked, "Will I be safe here and in Buffalo, sir?"

"I'll guarantee your safety, Josh. No need to worry," replied Reverend Mack.

Soon the steam railcar started up and they chugged along to Buffalo. It was getting late when they arrived at the port.

"Stay here while I check about the steamers leaving tonight," commanded the reverend.

As they sat together, Josh heard a man with a harsh voice say,

"There's one of them niggers, I bet, trying to escape to Canada." Josh put his head down but Seamus stood up and said boldly,

"He's a free man from Canada and we're all on our way home. You keep your hands off !"

When the two men scowled at them, the girls were concerned and Winnie questioned Josh, "What be they a'talking of, Josh?"

"They just think I'm a slave trying to get free because of my colour. Just don't anger them now Seamus," he added quietly. Fortunately, Reverend Mack returned to tell them that the Thames steamer was leaving within the hour. "This is the boat for us," he announced." It's built in Chatham and it's heading for Amherstburg and Detroit this night. Let's get on board." The two men tried barring their way but the reverend said, "We are all subjects of her majesty Queen Victoria. I will ask you only once to let us through." He sounded so full of authority that the two men backed away and the party of six headed for the Steamer.

"The captain will take us for steerage passage at $2.00 each. Do you have extra money, boys?" Reverend Mack asked.

"My da gave me some money to bring the girls back," said Seamus.

"And here's mine," said Josh, holding out two coins. "My uncle put money for me."

"Good. Now we can all get settled on board," replied the reverend. They all walked up the gang plank tired but happy to be closer to home.

"The officer said the girls can sleep inside this sheltered spot," Reverend Mack said, pointing to covered canvas. "Boys, here are two blankets for the night. I'll see you in the morning."

Seamus was so full of joy that he would have talked all night if Josh had let him. The young girls were soon soundly asleep. In the early dawn, Josh woke up to see the shores of Lake Erie in the distance. The boat was slowing to stop at a port. Within the hour, Seamus joined him. They watched the steamer dock at Port Stanley just as the girls came round to join them.

"Is this where we get off, Seamus?" Catherine inquired.

"No, indeed not. We have come a good way but have more to go still. We'll have some of this good bread and cheese now," he replied. Soon Reverend Mack came by with a jug of hot tea and two tin mugs. "Here you are. A fine morning, we're having! The captain says he's making good time. We'll make Amherstburg early tomorrow morning if all's well."

By noon they had loaded cargo and were off again. There was a decent wind and the captain had the sails up which made the boat go that much faster. Seamus played his tin whistle and Josh read the girls some of Longfellow's ballads from his book. Best of all they enjoyed looking out at the vast lake or watching the water curl away from the boat. The day was quiet and Winnie said,

"It's like a dream, Seamus, to be here with you and to feel safe with food in our bellies."

"When we get to Amherstburg, it will be a dream come true for my mam. She has been praying for this for months."

"After another night on board, we will be near our home town," said Josh.

Early the next morning, the boys were awake, straining their eyes to see the shore. Then they saw a familiar sight as the solid cement Bois Blanc lighthouse came into view. They were almost home!

"What an adventure we've had, Josh," exclaimed Seamus. "Look, there's the big Elliott house and the point on the other side." After a

An Unexpected Friendship

while, he went on to add, "See Josh, the mill's over there. Remember, that's where we first met."

"I won't ever forget that stone hitting my leg," teased Josh. "It was the best thing that ever happened 'cause it brought us together just when I needed a friend." He put his arm up and around his taller friend's shoulder.

Seamus smiled back and said, "That's for sure. Glad I am to have such a special friend like you. You've changed my life! I never expected to be so happy!"

"And you've made my life most interesting!" Josh added. Then both of them laughed together.

A Note about the people in this book

The story is centered around the relationship between two boys in 1846 when there was growing prejudice against Blacks in the town. The boys are completely fictitious but I used family names, I found in Amherstburg's census of 1841. James Alexander had a grocery store there and later became a miller. Peter Stokes was involved with Alexander and several other black men in the Coloured Militia of 1838. He became a Baptist lay preacher in Colchester. George McCoy who lived in the New Settlement was father of the famous Elijah McCoy who became an engineer on the railroad. He produced such a successful oil that the phrase, 'The real McCoy' became used for any genuine article.

The Harte girls were taken in by the Reverend Mack in October 1847. I just brought the date forward to that summer so that it would be good sailing weather. Steam ships were relatively new and people travelled by boat and rail en route to and from Toronto. The disastrous fire at the school actually happened in the winter of 1847.

Sarah Elliott was the widow of the famous Indian interpreter, Matthew Elliott who had been born in Ireland and who died in 1814. She lived as a widow for 54 years, dying in 1869. Her sons held respected positions in the district. Rev. Francis Gore Elliott was the rector of Christchurch, Colchester for 21 years; his brother, Robert was Amherstburg's treasurer until his death in 1858.

The Reverend Mr. Robert Peden was a cousin to James and John Dougall and the only teacher at the Dougall School. His views on salvation brought about his downfall in the Presbyterian Church in 1850. He left for Hamilton where he started the Evangelical Union Church.

James Dougall went on to become Mayor of Windsor and a prominent educator. He has a street and a school named after him in Windsor.

There are still Maloney and Hurst families living in Amherstburg. The map is based on those resident in the town in 1841. I used the fine map in the wonderful book, *Amherstburg 1776-1996*.

Reference Books

1. Amherstburg 1776-1996 : *The new Town on the Garrison Grounds* The Marsh Collection Society 1996
2. The Poems and Songs of Robert Burns on a web site.
3. Barry, James P. *Ships of the Great Lakes; 300 years of Navigation* Berkley Howell-North 1973.
4. Boyle, Harry J. *The luck of the Irish: a Canadian fable* Toronto: Macmillan of Canada, c1975.
5. Fradin, Dennis B *Bound for the North Star* Clarion Books New York 2000
6. Hollett, David *Packet Ships and Irish famine Emigrants 1845-51* Heaton Pub. Abergavenny, UK 1995
7. Lyons, Mary *Letters from a Slave Girl* (from writings of Harriet Jacobs) Scribner New York 1992
8. Mackay, Donald *Flight from Famine: Coming of Irish to Canada* McClelland & Stewart 1990
9. Nardo, Don *The Irish Potato Famine* Lucent Books 1990 series World Disasters
10. Schotter, Roni *F is for Freedom* Dorling Kindersley Publishing Inc. New York 2000
11. *Narratives of Fugitive Slaves* Accounts written in 1856, reprinted in 20th century.
12. Waterloo University has done wonderful research. As "*Immigration to Canada*", there is information about Irish immigration in 1847 and their plight. It is found on the site below:— http://ist.uwaterloo.ca.marj/genealogy/papers/children1847.html
13. I am grateful to Walter Lewis for information about steamers of the period at his web site:—http://www.hhpl.on.ca/GreatLakes/HomePort.asp

About the Author

Jane Buttery has written eight books, of which four are picture books. She also wrote two other novels for children and Portraits of An Orchestra about the Windsor Symphony musicians. In 2005, she produced an informative history of her local Anglican Church when it celebrated two hundred years. As a teacher, Jane saw the need to encourage reading about places children know in Ontario, Canada so she began writing about her area as soon as she retired.

With a UK degree in history, she enjoyed researching the 1830-47 period in the Western District of Upper Canada before producing this present novel. Jane is married with two daughters, two adult grandsons and one great-grand daughter. She lives in a rural area near Lake Erie about 15 km from Amherstburg and an hour's drive from Detroit, USA.